POPCORN

HOLLYWOOD STORIES

Also by Julia Cameron

NONFICTION
The Artist's Way
The Vein of Gold
The Right to Write
The Artist's Way Morning Pages Journal
Money Drunk/Money Sober (with Mark Bryan)
Heart Steps
Blessings
Transitions
The Artist's Way at Work (with Mark Bryan and Catherine Allen)
The Artist's Date Book
Supplies
God Is No Laughing Matter
God Is Dog Spelled Backwards

FICTION
The Dark Room

PLAYS
Public Lives
The Animal in the Trees
Avalon (a musical)
Four Roses
Love in the DM2
The Medium at Large (a musical)

POETRY
Prayers for the Little Ones
Prayers to the Nature Spirits
The Quiet Animal
This Earth

POPCORN

HOLLYWOOD STORIES

by

Julia Cameron

REALLY GREAT BOOKS

Requests for such permissions should be directed to:
Permissions Department
Really Great Books
P.O. Box 861302
Los Angeles, CA 90086

Library of Congress Cataloging in Publication Data
Cameron, Julia
Popcorn: Hollywood Stories
233 p. 13.335 x 20.32 cm.
ISBN 1-893329-12-7
1. Fiction 2. Hollywood 3. Film Industry
I. Title
II.
CIP 00-190813

Design by Ingrid Olson, Tülbox Studio
Printed in the United States of America
10 9 8 7 6 5 4 3 2 1

Really Great Books are available at special quantity discounts to use as premiums, for educational purposes, and/or sales promotions. For more information, please write to the Special Sales Department at the address above.

www.ReallyGreatBooks.com

Dedicated to the Great Director, for straightening out my plot lines, and to Julianna McCarthy, an actress to her fingertips.

Author's Note

I have lived my life at the movies. At the Liberty Palace with its swirled red velvet walls and creaky, cracked leather seats. At the Greenbay Theater, one town over, across the line, with its smell of stale perfume and popcorn, the odor of sex and sin.

That's where I saw my first B movie, as defined by the Catholic Church Legion of Decency. That is where the church and I parted company, right in the balcony. Sandra Dee gave her virginity to Troy Donahue and I gave mine to the movies.

For a woman of fallen virtue, I have been faithful. For two decades now I have written for and about the movies. The stories in this book are all my story. None of them is true, but all are accurate. I am a movie person, a movie writer. It's not so much a matter of character as of characters.

"You are a ventriloquist," a movie man once told me.

Maybe I am, but I'd have said I was the puppet and the movies made me dance.

What I will tell you is that I've danced with Sammy Davis, Jr., and made pasta for Bernardo Bertolucci. I've dined with Mr. Cukor and spent a stormy afternoon listening to Mr. Kurosawa say that not making movies almost killed him. In some other life, I will ask them if they remember. In this life, they were the stars and I was the bit player. Just as in "Mystic Canyon," I rounded out the scene.

The truth is, I made these stories up—or they made me up. You might call them "fiction" or "friction"—the abrasion of reality against dream. I suspect you will know some of these people and love some of them. So did I.

Julia Cameron
Taos, New Mexico
and
Venice, California.

CONTENTS

*The fact is I am quite happy in a
movie, even a bad movie. Other people,
so I have read, treasure memorable
moments in their lives: the time one
climbed the Parthenon at sunrise,
the summer night one met a lovely
girl in Central Park and achieved
with her a sweet and natural relationship,
as they say in books....
What I remember is the time John
Wayne killed three men with a carbine
as he was falling to the dusty street
in* Stagecoach, *and the time the
kitten found Orson Welles in the
doorway in* The Third Man.

—Walker Percy, *The Moviegoer*

POLITICALLY INCORRECT

Casting Call

[CRAFT SERVICE] With the boyish grace and the girlish glance, think young Hepburn—either one. Tender and streetwise, she's smart *and* smartass….LEAD (2) POSSIBLE NUDITY.

POLITICALLY INCORRECT

understand why she had to do it: politics.

"The world is the way it is," she told me. "We can't change that. We have to play ball. Doing anything else would be self-destructive." She had it all figured out. "I mean, I like to think I'm as honest as anyone else, but there are some things you just can't do. I mean, you could, but it could cost you *everything*...."

By "everything" she meant her career.

"Being gay is so difficult," she used to sigh to me. Often in bed. I would disagree. "It's the hiding it that's hard."

"Hiding is the easy part," she would counter.

For her, it would be. She was an actress to her fingertips—among other parts, it turned out. She acted straight and the world believed her. The look she gives her heroes on film would melt in your mouth, if not your hand. True romance with every single one of them. Everyone believes her—except me.

I knew the first day I met her. I was working craft service and one of the production assistants came over and said, "Something for Miss_____. Could you make brewed decaf with cinnamon in it, *right away?*" I said, fine, but not right away. I said, "I've got lunch break, two hundred guys, spaghetti or corned beef and cabbage, the brewed decaf will have to wait. Try Sanka."

I gave the P.A. two packets of Sanka. Then it was time to start dishing spaghetti. I wasn't trying to be wise or anything. Busy was just busy. I was dishing maybe plate fifty-five when all of a sudden these two packets of Sanka came at me on a plate.

"What the fuck is this?" a voice said, a voice that has launched a thousand accents. I looked up and it was Our Heroine.

"It's Sanka," I said. And I winked. I do that when I'm nervous.

"Did you wink at me?"

"I've got this twitch...." I shrugged.

"I asked for brewed decaf," she huffed. "Not this chemical shit. Some of us are careful what we put in our bodies." She looked me up and down like I was maybe not so careful about what I put in mine. Was she calling me a slut? Not and get away with it. Movie star or not, there were limits.

"This chemical shit is what I've got time for, doing spaghetti. If you don't get your panties in a ball, I'll get to the other right after lunch."

"In my trailer," she snapped. "Bring it to me yourself."

That's when I knew.

In her trailer, my ass. Our Heroine was looking at me like a snack. Did she think I was crazy? The caste system on a movie set makes India look liberated. She was a Star and I was an Untouchable. I planned to keep it that way and keep my job, thank you. I'd seen what happened to the trusting crew members who got involved with stars. "Snack" was putting it lightly.

Oh, I liked her on screen. The whole country did. She tends to take roles that involve saving the day. She plays the plucky woman who faces down the terrible monster. Movie to movie, the roles are the same, only the terrible monster changes—Nazism, the Mob, serial murderers of many stripes and, yes, social injustice in its Joseph's coat of many colors.

Role to role, she transforms her WASP self into whatever blue-collar person she's drawing to public attention. She specializes in playing downtrodden working-class girls. She calls it "rescuing them." I read somewhere that she "liked to do people that people would otherwise ignore." Does that mean me? I wondered.

There was no ignoring her, that's for sure. Not with her bone-china skin and candlelight-in-the-cathedral hair. Add to her looks her great talent and the even greater talent for finding out what the public wants and feeding it to them. With all her press, I have never read a negative word about her. She's the golden girl with the silver spoon and the platinum career.

Not me. I aim for worker among workers. I grew up in the business. I plan to grow old in the business. But not as an actress, thank you. Now, I've been told I bear a striking resemblance to the young Audrey Hepburn and maybe I do, if young Audrey Hepburn looked like an adolescent boy. Which is why it surprised me when she asked me out.

Which she did, over the brewed coffee, in her trailer.

"You're really interesting to me," she said.

"I'm interesting to me too."

"I'd really like to get to know you a little. It's good to have a friend on the set."

"So, hire one."

"I don't think that's funny. You have no idea how lonely I am. How lonely this is—" She gestured around her customized trailer. "Look, I didn't mean to be uppity before. I'm just nervous. The first day of a shoot is just agony for me—God, why am I telling you all this?"

It wasn't so much "why" she was telling me, as "how" she was telling me—her big blue eyes were pooling up with tears. I swear, they looked as big in person as they did up on the screen.

"Couldn't we at least go out to dinner? All my friends live in New York."

I invited her to my place, instead.

"I've got to feed the animals," I told her.

"Sounds exciting."

Little did she know.

I live high up in Topanga Canyon. I collect dogs, birds, cats, goats and the occasional exotic. The rule is they coexist peacefully.

My animals do. My house looks like a set for *Wild Kingdom*.

"What is this? A zoo?" Our Heroine said. She waved a hand at my cockatoo, my half dozen dogs and my twin Siamese. We were relaxing over a bottle of let's-seduce-each-other Chablis. Despite every caution I gave myself, I wanted her to stay the night. When she got off her high horse, she was actually hilarious. Only Lucy, my Australian shepherd, seemed oblivious to her charms.

"It's a long way back to town, isn't it?" she asked.

"Not so far."

"I probably shouldn't drive with the wine and all."

"The canyon's not that tricky."

"You really don't want me to stay, do you?"

"Your call."

I doubted she would—for one thing, I couldn't find Rosie, my boa constrictor. My eyes kept darting around the room, hoping to find the wily serpent.

"What are you looking for?" Our Heroine finally burst out in exasperation. This was not a woman accustomed to being ignored.

"My snake," I told her.

"Your *snake*?" (Rising inflection and volume.) "Most people are afraid of snakes—and, my God, the symbolism. I am a lesbian, after all."

I told her how gentle Rosie was, how warm to the touch, not cold and slimy.

"I happen to be deathly afraid of snakes. *Deathly*. How could you not tell me you kept a snake?"

That's when Rosie made her appearance, sliding quietly across Our Heroine's leg.

"Oh...my...God!" she exclaimed. (You have not seen terror until you have seen a movie star do it in the privacy of your own home.)

"Get...it...off...me."

"Her. Rosie. Her name is Rosie."

"Your snake."

"A rosy boa constrictor. She likes you, see? She's kissing your knee."

"What should I *do*?"

"Act like you like her. ACT."

ACT is a powerful word—to an actor, anyway. As I watched, Our Heroine stretched out a manicured hand and gave Rosie a friendly little pat. Rosie wiggled ecstatically.

"What's she doing now?"

"Saying thank-you."

"Really?"

"She's a fan."

Fan is another powerful word. Our Heroine gave Rosie a soothing stroke.

"Pretty girl," she crooned. "Does she like everyone?"

I had the sense to answer, "No."

Despite their genial introduction, Rosie spent that night sleeping in her terrarium, not looped across the bed. Our Heroine slept with me.

"I'm not usually so easy," she explained the next morning.

Easy? There were the down pillows to get rid of, the sheets to change "for luck," the darkening of all the windows, no easy task in a house with no curtains—and no neighbors, for that matter.

"Do you have *paparazzi* out here?"

"Mainly coyotes."

"I need privacy to relax," she explained.

"You mean to screw?"

"I hate that word."

"Fuck."

"I hate that more."

"Lady? No wonder you're a lesbian."

She laughed. It looked like we were going to have fun together after all.

With animals it's always a question of time and consistency. If you put in enough time and consistency, they will love you. I hate to say this, but with people it's exactly the opposite. Act fickle. Blow hot and cold. Pretend you could care less and they fall all over you.

I ignored Our Heroine the next day on set. She was ignoring me too, but that was to be expected. She was the star. I was craft service. At one point just before lunch rush—again—she sent an A.D. to ask for brewed decaf with cinnamon. I ignored the request. Let her suffer. Besides, I was doing shish kebab, one of our fancy entrees, and they took some assembling.

"Are you ignoring me?" There she was in the lunch line, just like real people.

"No, ma'am. I'm serving lunch. Shish kebab."

"I'll take a shit-ka-bob and brewed decaf."

"I'll get right on it," I lied.

Shish kebab is hell unless you have a long prep time—which I had spent in bed. A pineapple chunk, a cherry tomato, a mushroom cap, a green pepper slice, then chicken, steak, or lamb. Shish kebabs saved us a lot of money—all those vegetables and so little meat.

"Are they organic?" Still her. "We have to be careful what we put in our bodies."

"What? Are you organic?"

"The *vegetables*."

This was too much. The line behind her was sniggering. The reason she was lonely on set was because she was insufferable.

"I said, *Are they organic?*"

"Sure. If you shit them back out."

This contribution came from Shorty, the key grip. I don't think he meant Our Heroine to hear it, but she whirled on him.

"Are-you-talking-to-me?" she demanded. (Joan Crawford on a bad day, De Niro on a good one.)

Shorty got a rabbity look. "To her," he muttered, and pointed at me. As you might expect, Our Heroine had a certain reputation for sensitivity among crews. In other words, don't cross her.

"Hey! Leave me out of this."

"Then, get me my decaf," Her Highness said, and stamped back to her trailer. For all I knew, she would freak out about our night together and get me fired. I hopped right on the brewed decaf and delivered it myself.

"I hate crews," Her Highness was fuming as she slammed the trailer door behind me. "They love to see you fail. They live for the day you really blow it. Fart in a love scene. Anything. What's his name? That horrible little man in line. Who does he think he is?"

"One of the best grips in the business," I defended Shorty. My father had sponsored him into the union.

"He's vulgar. I suppose that's all you can expect from a grip."

This was crossing a line.

"My father was a grip."

"Oh...Is it too late to say I'm sorry?"

She gave me one of her Looks. This time it was contrition in bright blue neon. I wavered, but I wasn't buying.

"We're all vulgar," I told her. Let her fire me. "You're the one worrying about farting in a love scene."

Instead, she laughed.

"We are, aren't we?" She seemed relieved to drop the rock. "Do you know how exhausting it is to be a movie star? You can't fart. You can't do anything. It is excruciating. You can't possibly know."

"No. I'm just the lowly craft-service person. I could barely imagine. So, you wanted a shish kebab?"

"I want you."

We were Mutt and Jeff. Punch and Judy. The Odd Couple. To tell you the truth, I'd thought of me as a probable one-night stand for her. But we wound up playing house.

Our days went like this: up at dawn, feed the animals, return Rosie to the terrarium, drive to the set in different vehicles, arriving at staggered times. Feign indifference or polite acquaintance, grab each other over cinnamon decaf for five minutes after lunch. Leave separately and arrive home nearly simultaneously. She stopped for dailies. I stopped for groceries. Desire stopped for nobody.

Tiny little carrots. Crisp and lovely arugula. Snow peas. Scallops. Shiitake mushrooms, sun-dried tomatoes, goat cheese from my very own goats. Ah, love...nibble, nibble, nibble. Tumble to sleep exhausted. Repeat the performance, encore, encore, encore.

In short, I was back streets, but grateful. Love! Appearing live! Right here in Topanga Canyon. She was gaga over me too. (*Gaga* is her word.) I accepted the secrecy as part of the territory, a matter of professionalism. My father, a key grip for Ford, among other masters, had raised me with a movie ethic: Nothing, but nothing, must get in the way of the shoot. That included love, birth and death. Or, more often, given the nature of movie sets and location romance, the birth and death was love itself, which wrapped with the movie.

"I think secrecy gives our affair a frisson of eroticism," Our Heroine often informed me. I didn't agree, but I didn't disagree either. I was crazy about her.

Face it, being with a spiritual midget can be fun. To hear her tell it, her life was an endless series of woes and terrors. Wardrobe hated her. Makeup was out to do her in. The D.P. liked all the wrong angles. The director lacked sensitivity. The editor had claws for hands. I listened and laughed.

And a closet can be an erotic place—just like the bathroom in a jet. It's all a matter of imagination.

"Did I ever tell you I was a bisexual?" she said to me one night in bed.

"No."

"I was sure I had."

My heart thumped. Even the dogs heard it. Lucy, my Australian shepherd, had never liked her. I swear to you, she growled at this remark. Our Heroine jumped.

"Why is she growling at me?"

"Don't worry," I told her. "That's just her early warning growl."

"Mmm. What was I saying?"

"You were saying you liked to do it with guys."

"I couldn't have put it that way. I meant I like men."

"Sure. Me too."

"I'm serious."

"So am I. I just don't like to fuck them."

"How would you know?"

She had a point. I never had slept with a man. I was the young protégée of an older Phys Ed teacher. A gay cliché, I know, but it had stopped my heterosexual career in its tracks. Whatever curiosity I had was quickly snuffed out by gay politics. Bisexuals were politically despicable in the circles I traveled in. So were "hasbians," lesbians who couldn't stand the heat of radical living and crawled back to the heterosexual hearth. Not me, I'd vowed. And so, to me, men remained terra incognita. Whiskers, muscles, penises—it all seemed impossibly exotic.

"Look, why are you telling me this?"

"What do you mean?"

"About liking men. Is there something I should know?"

"I don't think so."

Of course she didn't think so. She was Miss Secrecy, queen of the closet and the "erotic frisson" of a double life. I spent a fitful night.

"What's wrong with this dog?"

It was five A.M., a rosy dawn in Topanga Canyon. Our Heroine was tugging at one end of an indigo bra. Lucy was tugging at the other.

"She likes you," I lied. "She thinks you're playing."

"I think she's hostile. It's my favorite bra. I stole it from wardrobe."

"Instant karma."

"Shut up."

"Lucy! Drop it!" I said this in a thunderous tone.

Lucy dropped it. The delicate indigo lace hung in shreds.

"Bad dog," Our Heroine scolded. Lucy snapped at air.

"Why is she so hostile?"

"She's a militant lesbian dog. She heard you say you're bisexual. Now, you tell me."

"I told you last night. Besides, what difference does it make?"

We would soon find out.

Forgive me if I call him Rock. As in, *got his rocks off.* As in, *dropped the rock on my head.* As in, *ouch!* It's not his real name, but men always choose extreme pseudonyms.

You'd know him from the tabloids. From the big and little screens. Maybe even from the footlights. Rock started out with country-star fame, added soap-opera fame and then made a crossover success in an action–adventure movie with lots of bare-chested action shots and an unlikely subplot about his singing talents. In short, Rock was a near star. Soon to be a big star. He just needed a small boost to really make it....A little affair with Our Heroine would give him just the boost he needed.

I was serving lasagna. (My mango chutney was considered too

exotic for a crew.) I had my back to the window, changing trays, when I heard her.

"I just *love* lasagna, don't you?" Our Heroine doing a little fake voice.

"Yeah, sure. If it's good." A real macho bass, not hers.

I spun around. There they were, arm in arm, Rock and Our Heroine.

"Dining with the commoners?" It was out before I knew it.

"I don't see any commoners around here." She patted his arm.

"Two lasagna? With meat?"

"The only way," Rock volunteered.

"The only way," she cooed up at him. So much for her vegetarian ethics.

"Coming right up."

What was coming right up was my stomach. Ever the obedient galley slave, I shoveled two gigantic portions for them. Rock reached for both plates.

"Thank you," she breathed. To Rock, not to me. I almost lost it in the lasagna.

"Smells great." Rock grinned at me, right out to the canines. He had nice teeth and nicer eyes—merry, like a husky's.

Driving home from location I took the Ventura Boulevard exit to stop at the newsstand. There they were in living color: Rock and Our Heroine. A hot new tabloid romance. I bought *Star*, *The Globe* and *The National Enquirer*. I drove home using twisting back roads and got home early anyway. I spread the tabloids on the kitchen table.

THE REEL THING, LIFE IMITATES ART, the headlines read. Rock looked at her with lust in his heart and she looked at him with blind adoration. *Marriage in the works?* the subhead read.

"Look at this shit, Rosie," I said, lifting her from her terrarium. I touched the groove under her snout. She hissed obligingly.

"Right. They're villains. Right?"

I draped Rosie around my neck and settled in at the table for a good cry. The cry lasted two minutes. I wasn't sad, I was angry. "Fuck being fucked over," I told Rosie. "I'm not taking this." Rosie licked my cheek. She gave me a little hug—not always affection from a boa constrictor. I put her back in her terrarium. Home sweet home. I began making dinner. Lasagna again. Lugged home in my trunk. No more tenderly sautéed organic midget carrots. No more snow peas and cashews. I felt like a carnivore. She wants to trade my candlelit meals and my love nest for a tabloid star? Exit candlelit dinners, exit love nest.

I was slamming pans and generally making a good, solid din. "I'm home, honey." A wee peeping cry amid the crashing pots. Our Heroine acting innocent. Acting, period.

"Let me try another reading. I am home, *honey!*" This was serious and Our Heroine knew it. She pulled out all the stops, coming up behind me to nibble first at my ear, then the dinner.

"Big deal."

"Oooh. You're mad at me."

"Of course I'm mad at you. What was that?"

"It's business. You know that."

"Does he know that?"

"Well, I assume so."

"Does he know about us?"

"God, I hope not. I barely know him. Why is Rosie still in her terrarium?"

"She might bite someone."

"Rosie doesn't bite...does she?"

"Rosie can be trained."

"Don't be jealous." Nibble, nibble. "This lasagna has meat in it!"

"What's the big deal? So did you."

"Don't be vulgar."

"I was referring to your lunch," I lied.

"Oh. You didn't think I ate it, did you?"

"I don't know what you do with one of those."

"You are so paranoid."

"Maybe."

I put in the garlic bread. Tossed the salad. Set the table. Our Heroine hovered like a hummingbird the whole time. Fine. If she chose to act innocent, I chose not to tell her of my plan.

I have never, in all my life, been interested in a man, except as a friend. But men have always been interested in me. My theory is that men are interested in anything they can't have: Mt. Everest, the sound barrier, girls like me.

The next day on the set I wore a leather bustier, a fake tattoo on my biceps and a button that read *Lavender Love*. When Rock came through the lunch line (chicken Creole), I gave him a flash of cleavage.

"Like my lasagna?" I asked.

"Loved it." He liked my breasts too.

"Tell me what you like and I'll feed it to you," I promised. "I saved you a tray of that lasagna."

"That's sweet."

"No way, baby. Read my tit."

I leaned across the table to show him my *Lavender Love*. He was astonished. I wasn't his idea of a bull dyke.

"You're not *really*?"

"Oh, yes. *Really*. You expected combat boots? I have a very attractive pair. And some lovely camouflage gear to wear them with, whenever I want to keep a low profile. Yes, *really*."

"My loss. Well, you still smell good," he said. (I'd borrowed a blast of Our Heroine's perfume.)

"Mush," I told him. "It was something in the baby formula."

"Hello, you two!" It was Our Star. She was not pleased by our camaraderie. "Rock, want to eat lunch with me?"

"I was telling her she had great lasagna—"

"But you were thinking I had great tits."

"Busted. You do have great tits."

"We *all* have great tits," Our Heroine harrumphed.

"Can I get you anything?" I asked. Rock, not her.

"I would take some of that lasagna."

"I'll bring it to you."

"Thanks. I'll be in my trailer."

I turned to my pots and pans. I heard Our Heroine huffing and puffing behind me.

"I—can't—believe—you—would—do—this—to—me," she hissed.

"Do what?"

"Pretend to like him."

"But he's a doll! You like him yourself....Sanka?"

I handed her a cup of tepid decaf. Then I handed her the bombshell. "Maybe I'm bisexual," I told her.

"This is bullshit."

I couldn't have agreed more.

"Maybe you really are bisexual," Rock volunteered two nights later over dinner. We'd wrapped early and he'd stopped by craft service to return my lasagna pan. One thing (my leather bustier) led to another (a dinner invitation) and two hours later we were dining in Santa Monica, in a swank eatery on Ocean Boulevard.

"You remind me a little of Audrey Hepburn," he said. "You're really beautiful, you know that?"

"I'll bet you say that to all the girls."

"Actually? They all say that to me." He sounded wistful.

We were sitting at a window table and a light breeze ruffled his hair. He *was* beautiful, even I could see that. He had ink-black hair and light blue eyes—like a husky or John Travolta.

What's worse, he was fun. He laughed at my jokes. By the time we were only halfway through a carafe, I found myself telling him tales from the crypt—memories of my childhood, indentured to the movies.

Of course, they were really Dad's memories more than mine, but they were the bedtime stories of my youth: the time Ford made an actor out of a wrangler, remarking, "If he can ride that well, acting should be easy. It's the same trick—don't let yourself get thrown."

Then it was my turn to listen to Rock's stories of West Virginia white lightning and tent revivals, biscuits and gravy, pickup trucks and shotguns. We spent a good half hour on hunting dogs alone, blue tick, coon, you name it. I told him about my dog Lucy, about the way Lucy had of sorting people out.

"You can't fool children or dogs," Rock advised me gravely.

The waiter brought a second carafe of wine. We clinked glasses. Rock looked at me with his merry husky's eyes.

"You remind me of a dog," I informed him, "a husky."

"Mush," he replied.

I was having too much fun, I suddenly realized. I was forgetting my agenda. At the moment, I couldn't even remember my agenda. This was a bad sign.

"You're not laughing," Rock observed solemnly.

My agenda snapped back into focus. My God! What was I doing?

"What's so funny about trying to seduce your girlfriend's boyfriend?" I blurted out.

"What? Who's doing that?"

"I am."

"What?"

"Our Heroine. Your girlfriend. She's *my* girlfriend. And she's playing both sides against the middle. Don't you get it? I'm only out with you to teach her a lesson."

Rock blinked. "Hey. Don't sugarcoat it. I can take my medicine like a man."

Maybe he could, but what he looked like was Lucy right after she'd been scolded.

"I was starting to think you liked me," I explained.

"I do like you."

"It was making me feel uncomfortable. Not honest."

"Good. I'd hate to think you were completely ruthless."

We were at an impasse. He liked me and I did like him. This was not good news to a confirmed lesbian. For years I had heard stories of wishy-washy bisexuals, of lesbians who couldn't stand the heat. Politically, such sexual vacillation was viewed with contempt. Not me, I'd vowed.

"I can't like you," I told him. "It's politically incorrect."

"Maybe you're bisexual."

"Nope."

"Well then, what do you want for dinner?"

What was it with this man?

Rock and I talked until two A.M. I drank more than I had in years and enjoyed it. Rock couldn't imagine growing up in the movie business. His town didn't even have a movie theater. I couldn't imagine the Appalachians.

"Movies were as foreign to us as—"

"Lesbians in leather bustiers?"

"Nah. Those were a dime a dozen."

"Mmm."

"Say that again."

"Mmm."

Suddenly, he leaned over and kissed me. I liked his mouth even though it was edged with bristles. He licked my lip and so I licked his. His lower lip felt like a Barcalounger. I could have stayed there forever. Oh, my God, maybe—

"It's the wine," he said. "Don't worry."

The waiters were staring daggers. It was time to go home, not make public displays of affection. We paid the bill, left and crossed the street to Palisades Park.

"I don't understand this," I told him, standing hipbone to hipbone under the stars. We were just at the railing where the cliff fell away to the dark Pacific.

"What's to understand?"

"I was just using you. You were a pawn. If it worked, she's madly, miserably in love with me. Actually, I should go home and find out."

"I have a better idea. Come to my house. Let me spend the night with you. Maybe I'm miserably in love with you."

"You're not miserable."

"No. I'm not. Come here." He reached for me and his arms suddenly seemed infinitely more dangerous than the cliff we were standing on. I put a hand on his chest and backed off.

"No way. Bad enough I've got a pissed-off girlfriend and a lonely boa constrictor."

"Bad enough," Rock agreed. "*A boa constrictor?*"

"Rosie. My father gave her to me when I said I wanted to be an animal wrangler. He thought she would change my mind."

"And? Make you like penises?"

"No! Scared me off animal wrangling, but I liked her. If anything will keep me from being an animal wrangler, it's cooking."

"Maybe you could make animal cookies."

"Maybe we should go home."

"Think about it. You love to cook. I love to eat. It's a match made in heaven."

"Rock. We are not a match. I am a militant lesbian feminist. This is a ploy. I was using you, to make my lover jealous."

He moved my hand to one side, leaned down and kissed me. Even with the little bristles, it was quite a kiss.

"Rock. This is not politically correct. I—I despise bisexuals—I think they're lying to themselves. I have never—"

He kissed me again. Had the jacaranda smelled so sweet all evening?

"This is still politically incorrect. What about— It's cheating!"

"C'mon," he said. "She did it to you."

"That was politics," I snapped. "Politics make strange bedfellows. She didn't want to sleep with you. She just wanted the tabloids to say she did. You know, for her career."

Rock held me at arm's length and looked me in the eyes.

"Right. And I'm only kissing you to make your lover jealous."

The big son of a bitch. Triangulating me and my lover. This was probably how he got his male chauvinist rocks off, the bastard. And I'd been dumb enough to think he actually liked me.

"Hurt you, didn't I?"

"Yes. Satisfied?"

"I didn't actually sleep with her."

"But?"

"She's a great actress but some things are pretty tough to fool. Like Henry."

"Henry?"

"My cock. He was not fooled. She was not interested. I did not sleep with her."

"You didn't?" Relief rushed over me. The inky Pacific seemed ruffled by breezes. "Oh, I'm so glad you didn't sleep with her."

"Did you hear what you said? You said you were glad *I* didn't sleep with *her*."

"So?"

"So, I'm the one you care about. Otherwise you would have said you were glad *she* didn't sleep with *me*."

He was right and I knew it.

A definite wind rustled the palm trees. A single large frond broke free and floated out, wind-tossed, beyond the railing, to settle like a giant feather on the restless sea. Was a storm coming on? When had the waves changed tempo, become so ominous?

"I meant vice versa," I protested lamely. "I have to go. Thank you for a lovely evening."

"Look," he said. "She's a movie star. She did what she had to do to get there. She'll do what she has to do to stay."

"That's why she's in the closet," I told him. I was chilled.

"That's the point. If she thought it would help her career, she'd come straight out."

"No way. Dream on." I felt dizzy. It was either too much wine or too much reality.

"Let me take you home, you look wiped."

"I feel *something*."

I declined Rock's offer of a ride. I drove home through Santa Monica Canyon, each turn unfolding a surprise to me. I was not entirely sober. The wine, I told myself, the wine is making all things new.

I should have seen it coming. I arrived home that night to find a drunk movie star sprawled across my bed.

"I hope you're satisfied," she snarled, almost mid-snore. A bottle of Kahlua stood empty by the bed. The phone was off the hook and next to it was a list of phone numbers, each one helpfully identified: *People, The Globe, The National Enquirer, Star*— What had she done? I wondered.

"What's your call?" I tried to rouse her. "What time do you have to be on set?"

"Mmm. Late," she muttered, curling back into sleep.

I tried again to rouse her. No doing, and just as well. I had an early call the next morning. I had to be at the Farmers Market before dawn or we'd have wilted vegetables for our Provençale. I set my alarm and fell into an oddly exhilarated sleep. I woke up, donned camouflage, combat boots and lipstick—don't ask me why—and I drove, *singing*, to the set.

I arrived at the studio gate at 5:30 A.M. I felt fine and worried that I should have felt much worse. My voice to God's ear.

"There she is! There she is!"

I heard the reporters before I saw them. I slid my pickup into its spot and was just setting out my bags of produce from the Farmers Market when they landed on me.

"You're the lover, aren't you?"

"What?"

"Her lover. You're the lesbian lover."

"I—?"

"You see? She is! Oh, I think it's so brave of her coming out! I *really* admire her! And I bet it helps her career."

These optimistic sentiments poured from a crew-cut blonde whose press ID read "R.A.G.E." I had seen him at Gay Pride rallies for years.

"You work in craft service, is that correct? And your name is spelled—?"

"Wait a minute!" I shouted. "What is this?"

A momentary lull in the noise greeted my question. Finally, a lanky young man in a rumpled Armani suit answered my question. "It should be obvious, darling! You've been outed."

"Great," I said. "I've got to get to work."

With that, I shouldered my produce bags and pushed my way through the reporters, photogenic as a young bear. Fortunately, it was a chicken Provençale day on the set and I could Provençale in my sleep.

Chop the leeks, mince the garlic, stew the tomatoes...

"Surviving?" It was Rock, somewhere between the leek soup and ratatouille.

"I could kill her," I replied. "And I will if this publicity doesn't. Why would she out herself? Do you think she was in a blackout? She was drunk as a skunk when I got home."

I told Rock about the Kahlua, the list of phone numbers, the drunken sprawl.

"I hope she's okay," I added.

"She's fine. You're the one in jeopardy," he said ominously.

"What do you mean?"

"She's having a field day at a press conference right now."

"What?"

Just then a production assistant approached. "Producer wants to see you," he told me.

Our producer was Alden Spengler, a nice producer, if there is such a thing. Happily married thirty years. A rare breed.

"Why'd you do it?" he asked when I stepped inside his office. Spengler favored crisp Turnbull & Asser shirts, today's in a mint and white stripe.

"I'm sorry, sir?"

"You think I didn't know about you two? I've been in the business too long to miss a thing like that—even if it's extremely discreet. And you were."

"Thank you."

"*Were*, I said. Now this fiasco, how could you?" Spengler looked genuinely grieved.

It slowly began to dawn on me. Spengler thought I called the press.

"Wait a minute. All I did was go out to dinner with a friend," I protested. "I didn't do anything."

"Who? What friend?"

"Rock."

"That putz. First her, then you. Can't he keep his dick in

his pants?" Spengler ran his hands through his closely barbered hair. He really did look terrible. "That putz!" he repeated.

"Rock didn't sleep with her. It was politics. She needed a romance to up her stock." Why was I defending Rock?

"Well, she's certainly got one now. Lesbian lovers! Do you think that helps our movie?" He was shouting, a scary thing from a quiet man like him. I could feel tears stirring in my eyes.

"Don't cry!" he thundered. "Think!"

There was a knock at the door. It was Our Heroine. Or, at least, her screen persona.

"Imagine meeting you here," she snapped. She gave me a glare of scorn normally reserved for her Nazi inquisitors on film.

"What did you tell them?" Spengler asked her. "I thought it was best to stay out of sight."

"I told them," Our Heroine looked directly at me, her every fiber quivering with righteous indignation, "that she was lying. I said her phone calls were a desperate grab for attention."

"What?" I felt my hearing go, replaced by the funny wah-wah-wah of shock. "My phone calls? I never!"

"About our affair—our alleged affair."

"Anything else?" Spengler was talking to her.

"Yes, I said she was a radical lesbian feminist with a political agenda. I said she was obsessed," she went on. "I said she was trying to smear me—"

"That's good," Spengler told her. "Good girl." Then he turned to me. "Sorry, sweetheart. I know your father would understand. This is business. I think we should talk about terminating your services."

"I'm the scapegoat here?" I squeaked.

"I'm afraid so," Spengler admitted. "Unless you've got another way to handle it."

"Of course I do—I mean, I love my job!"

"I know that, sweetheart, and I'm sorry. I loved your dad and I love your chicken Provençale. But what else can I do?"

"Anything!"

"I'm afraid not."

"But she—"

"She's the star."

Spengler looked resolved but troubled. His first concern was the film's safety, of course, but he *had* always liked me—and especially my chicken Provençale.

There was a knock on the door. Spengler ignored it, but the door opened with a burst. It was Rock, looking angry.

"You putz!" Spengler snapped. "Couldn't keep your dick in your pants! Maybe it's okay in Nashville, but here in Hollywood, we have standards!"

Rock ignored him. I was quaking in my combat boots. Our Heroine feigned disinterest. She made an elaborate show of crossing to the window to stare out at a passing golf cart. Rock crossed to her side, took her by one arm and swung her around. "I know what you did," he told Our Heroine. "And I know why you did it."

"Why did she do it?" Spengler bit.

"She heard about our wedding plans."

"What?" (Our Heroine.)

"What?" (Me.)

"I'm in love with her," Rock explained to Spengler, who thought he meant Our Star.

"Strange way to show it, dining out with another girl." (For a Hollywood producer, Alden Spengler could be very straitlaced.)

"Not *her*." Rock nodded from Our Heroine, who was looking appalled, to me. "*Her*. I just told them."

"Me?" I was still lead-footed on the uptake.

"You told the press what?" Our Heroine hissed.

"That I loved her. That I was trying to marry her. That you were obsessed with me and could not let go."

"Now, there's a plot." Our Heroine was not amused.

Spengler was a quick study. His woe gave way to fatherly warmth.

"A jealous spat? Between two girls? Over you?"

"Exactly."

"Young man, you're brilliant!" Spengler clasped his hands above his head in Rocky's victory salute. "Brilliant. They'll love it."

"I hate it," Our Heroine announced. "Why do I have to be the bitch?"

"I don't know," he told her. "Maybe it's genetic."

"What do *you* think?" Rock asked me.

"Pretty smart," I allowed. Rock's eyes twinkled. He looked like the dog who knew how to play fetch. I felt more than ever like an animal lover.

Spengler leaned across the desk and took my hand. "Please," he begged. "Do it for me. Marry him. You can always have it annulled later. Think of what your father would have done. Please. Help me out. Do it for the movie. It's politics."

Politics make strange bedfellows, but no stranger than a rosy boa constrictor, a West Virginia hillbilly and a radical lesbian feminist (reformed).

I told Rock I'd marry him. To save the movie.

Sex with a man is a lot like mango chutney—an acquired taste that can certainly become an addiction.

"A happy ending," Rock teases me. Our wedding was a blissful year ago. "She's with that comedienne—she may yet come out —and you're with me. We're all happy. Just like in the movies."

"Nonsense," I tell him. "I'm just a lesbian. I'm in denial. I can't possibly be happy. That would be politically incorrect. I'm thinking of making some mango chutney."

THE VOICE

Casting Call

[THE STUDIO HEAD] A big bear, jocular, sardonic, likable and a lug….LEAD (28)

The Voice

"I hate talent," I've been widely quoted as saying. I never said it. The real quote goes "I hate the talent." By that I mean writers, actors, directors, mainly actors. You would too, in my position. You think it's easy running a studio?

The salary. I'll bring that up before you do. I make more money than I could possibly spend and that's fine. In this town, it gets me respected. Or what passes for respect: groveling and fear. You see a lot of groveling and fear when you're the cheese. And, running a certain studio, I am the cheese.

My wife says she fucks me out of pity. That's why I married her. She makes me laugh, and she's right, that's how hard my job is. At my salary, I shouldn't complain, but I do every day from four to four-fifty on a protected line to my shrink. Yesterday I told him, "Harrison Bourke is making a run for my job. I think I'll let him have it."

"Now, why would you do that?" my shrink wondered.

"So I could watch an otherwise perfectly competent, even brilliant man make a fool of himself," I snapped, still smarting I suppose from Bourke's comments to the press about my animated musical, *Medea*.

"I'd like to think I'd have known better," Harrison told *Variety*, meaning, I told my shrink, that he doubtless would have done *Oedipus* instead. We all have our blind spots. I try not to have too many people standing in mine.

"All I want is a little dignity," I tell my wife.

She laughs at me. "Then don't tell anybody about Walt," she tells me.

"You and Harry."

"You told Harry?"

"He's my shrink."

"What did Harry say?"

"He said we all have our coping devices."

"Pardon me, but it seems to me the ghost of Walt Disney is a lot more than just a coping device."

"You think I'm crazy?"

"Well, I think you're imaginative."

"How many times do I have to tell you, I'm *not* making it up?"

"I know, I know." My wife put on the special patented voice she had for talking to me about my business difficulties.

That's why I married her. Unlike the rest of this town, she found worrying about movies, even thinking about movies, somewhat silly. I guess when I told her about Walt it seemed no crazier than spending $82 million to build an animated tarantula for our box-office smash, *Spider*. I was right about that one. I knew people would go see a good-enough movie about bugs. Of course, if I'm honest, I should admit it really was Walt's idea.

I had just completed the Japanese rock garden outside my office, an idea inspired by my friend Ken Wilber, lover of all things Zen. He was a genius—is a genius—and I was hoping that some of it might rub off. I try to be open-minded about spiritual matters, of course I do. My salary is miracle enough. So, I built the rock garden with its wandering lagoons of koi, its miniature waterfalls, its imported cherry trees and curved stone benches for meditation. Sure, it felt a little pretentious, but I was willing to try anything for a little peace of mind—and anything included Zen meditation gardens as well as daily conversation with Harry on the protected line. To tell you the truth, instead of making me feel tranquil, the place did strike me as spooky—it's unnaturally quiet, except for the *drip drip drip* of water down the faces of carefully cantilevered slabs of stone.

"Nice garden" was the first I'd heard from Walt. I was sitting on one of my meditation benches, killing time before my call to Harry. "Nice garden," a voice said, and I whipped my head around to see who was talking. It was a familiar voice, with more than a little Midwestern twang. I recognized the twang because my masseur had it, and he was from Omaha.

"Smart move," the Voice continued approvingly. "How about a movie about bugs?" Now I knew I *was* crazy. At the mention of bugs, I suddenly imagined a terrifying spider, crouched behind the very pile of cantilevered rocks where I was sitting. "Tarantula." The word rang out in the same twangy voice. I did know the voice. This is one for Harry, I thought. He'll get a kick out of this one.

"Not everything is rational," the Voice picked up. "You should know that. What's rational about a talking duck or a long-term romance between two rodents in bobby socks?" He had a point. By then, I was thinking of the Voice as "him," and I even had a dim suspicion *which* "him." How many times had I watched the old footage of a man in love with his work, overseeing every step of the creative process from the first tentative sketches to the final brilliant results? Always, in cozy retrospect, his ideas looked brilliant. But they must have sounded harebrained at the time. An animated Tchaikovsky? Who would rush to see that? And yet we had.

"Bugs," the Voice whispered. "Relax. They're a good idea."

The alarm on my Rolex sounded. So much for meditation. The "bug" that was bugging me now was whether or not my protected line to Harry was truly protected. Not to be paranoid, which I clearly was, but "our gang," as I referred to the clubhouse mentality of my competitors, had taken to racing ideas into production that were remarkably similar to my own projects. I only hoped bugs would be safe from thievery. And so, I shook off my first encounter with the Voice and retreated to my office, to my $5,000 glove-leather chair, where I called Harry and complained about my tax bill.

"You've got a real problem there," Harry humored me. "You'll barely have enough money left to buy Las Vegas."

"Harry," I said, "I just had a horrifying thought. What if this phone is bugged?"

"I thought you had it swept once a week."

"I do, I do. But what if—"

"That's why you're good at your job," Harry interrupted me. "You're good at playing 'what-if.'"

"Thanks, Harry." It did help, the knack he had—a trick, really — of casting the most negative situations in a positive light. Take the time my prize director sexually assaulted a minor.

"Good for business," Harry told me. "The public loves to see a squeaky-clean company like yours get its toe caught in a mousetrap."

"I'll pardon that expression. I'm worried about something else. I've got a dyke movie star and Baby cast as Beverly Hills bank robbers. I'm worried they'll have an affair and we'll never live it down."

"Of course they'll have an affair," Harry said in his most soothing tone. "Why worry about it?" That's what I loved about Harry. He was good at the bottom line—almost as good as I was.

I remember it was raining slightly the next day, the sort of fine mist they get in San Francisco but seldom in the San Fernando Valley. I left my goatskin Calvin Klein butter-yellow jacket in the lap of my overstuffed mitt of a chair. Slipping one of my logo sweatshirts over my head, I felt quite monklike, slipping out the sliding door to my waiting garden.

"Hire the kid." I heard his voice as soon as my bony butt made contact with the slick, damp stone bench.

"I will, I will," I spoke out loud. I could always pretend I was talking to the fish if some wayward gardener encountered me. "The kid" was a hot young female director who'd made a splash on the indie circuit with a documentary about her cowboy husband and his horse, Buck. Who better to direct our remake of *Annie Oakley, Cowgirl*? Of course, we'd tinkered with the story a little—we always do. Annie was younger and prettier than Annie had ever been, and rumor had it—accurate, as always—that Julia was interested, but only if we went with Charles—that moody pain-in-the-ass—as her costar. I was slumping into depression just thinking about it all. You know your life is out of kilter when Annie Oakley gets you depressed.

"Trigger," the Voice said.

"You're right. I could shoot myself."

"No, no," the Voice chided. "Get her a good horse, one like Trigger, that kids will remember."

Kids, it always came back to his goddamn kids. He was right about that. He was right about almost everything, I came to think over the next few months when our daily chats became a matter of habit. So far, I'd avoided telling Harry. My one discretionary area, you might say. I was on the verge of confessing, when the news broke about New Age guru Jean Houston urging Hillary Clinton to gain wisdom and perspective through imaginary chats with Eleanor Roosevelt.

"Do you think that's crazy?" I asked Harry, referring to the First Lady's tête-à-têtes.

"Whatever works," Harry answered.

It was my opening. Now or never.

"I do something similar every afternoon," I began.

"You do, don't you," Harry interrupted, referring, of course, to our standing appointment.

"Yeah, yeah, I do." I let the moment pass.

The next afternoon the Voice applauded my reticence. "It's good to have a few secrets," the Voice piped up just as I was watching a cruising battalion of koi round a mossy rock and slide from view. "Secrets help," the Voice continued. "People love secrets."

"Boo!" I said.

The Voice chuckled, "Boo who?"

I had two simultaneous ideas. One was for a ghost story, the other was for a comedy called *Shrinks*. I could use midgets. They could ride in backpacks, wisely advising their bearers.

"Hold on a minute there," the Voice advised. "I'd run that one past Harry."

And so, that afternoon—moments later, really—I found myself telling Harry about the voice and the juvenile fear I had—sibling rivalry, really—that if Harrison Bourke got my job the Voice would talk to him.

"It sounds like you need to have a heart-to-heart," Harry counseled me.

"With Harrison Bourke?" I gasped. "No one in known history has survived one of those."

"Not with Harrison. With *him*."

Although Harry didn't say the name, I knew Harry was thinking it.

"Shhh," I hushed him. "I'll think about it."

The next afternoon was one of those perfect days that come about ten times a year. Yesterday's rain had scrubbed the dirty window, and the mountains, jagged and majestic, came into view. I could imagine my little garden was flanking Mount Fuji. I could imagine I was talking to Walt.

"Good to see you, son," the Voice said gently as soon as I was settled on my bench. "I'm sorry you're worrying. I'm sorry it's so hard."

That's when the tears started; round and plump like cartoon tears, they welled up and spilled over, streaking my hangdog cheeks. Goddamn it, it was hard. My health showed that, didn't it? It was hard.

Cherry blossoms blew through the air as a soft breeze rippled the surface of the koi pond.

"Son," the Voice spoke again softly, "I'm proud of you, son." The tears spilled down in earnest then, as I realized I'd never even told Harry about the burden of his legacy and the child's need I had to make him proud.

HEROIN, WITH AN E

Casting Call

[ALEXANDER] A Brit, with that patented, ambiguous—yet withholding—sexual smolder that keeps American women flocking to the movie theaters. He wouldn't kick Hollywood out of bed, but he'd hate to admit chasing her....LEAD (36) POSSIBLE NUDITY.

HEROIN, WITH AN E

The first time I met Glennis, she was living in Laurel Canyon with Richmond Egley, the record producer, and practicing a maintenance diet of wheat grass and heroin. You had to see her to believe her: milk-white skin, eyes the blue of sapphires, hair so pale, so baby fine, it looked translucent. Richmond made the introductions.

"Alexander, Glennis. Glennis, Alexander."

"Nice name." Glennis smiled up from under her cloud of wispy hair. She toyed with a silken ribbon tying it back.

"Yours or mine?" I asked. She laughed at that, a high, silvery sound like tiny bells.

I was in Los Angeles because my agent thought the time was right. "You can cross over," he told me. "You can be a really big international star, not just the darling of the West End." (This was what every London stage actor longed to hear.) Crossing over—from England to America; from stage to film—meant big money and, my agent told me, "didn't need to mean compromise."

I loved Los Angeles. Palm trees. Sprinklers. Girls like Glennis. She dressed in white eyelet except for her hair ribbons, which alternated pink, blue or lavender, according to her moods: happy, sad, variable.

"Do you like me?" Glennis asked.

"She's very direct," Richmond said.

"We've just met," I stalled.

"He likes me," Glennis announced. She abandoned Richmond's arm and moved to mine. Richmond shrugged and smiled at her fondly. What next? I wondered.

"Want to check out the hot tub?" Glennis asked. She was unbuttoning the bodice of her little white eyelet dress.

"Go ahead," Richmond urged. Glennis was unbuckling my belt. I grabbed my trousers.

"Richmond's very understanding," Glennis said. Both of them laughed.

"Can't! Got an audition!" I managed to pant.

"You mean a 'meeting,'" Glennis corrected me. She laughed like those tiny temple bells. I felt hopelessly carnal. Did people "hot tub" like shaking hands?

"I'm friendly. That's all," Glennis explained, taking in my alarm and moving back to Richmond.

"I'm British," I blurted out. Whatever that meant.

"Rub my back, Richmond. I'm so sore." She shrugged her bodice from her shoulders to reveal two perfect breasts. Richmond winked at me and began kneading her shoulders.

"I'll take a rain check on that hot tub," I told them. I let myself out.

Auditions in Los Angeles range from "meetings" where they look you over, to "meetings" where they listen to you read, to "meetings" where they listen to you think. Since I was British and Hollywood remains incurably Anglophilic, I tended to have the third kind. What is it about a British accent that makes Americans assume you are smart? I was asked my thinking on everything from death by cancer (*Doomed Love*, a major studio release) to life as an alien in Congress ("Sort of *Mr. Martian Goes to Washington*," an independent feature). Lastly, at all the meetings, I was asked how I liked Los Angeles.

"Love it," I always said. "Great weather, great girls."

"You meet Glennis yet?" I was asked that very afternoon. My audition was for a sensitive, doomed young lover ("Sort of Romeo in intensive care").

"Richmond Egley's girl? Matter of fact, I did meet her.

This afternoon."

"Great girl, eh? She's our Juliet." Glennis was cast as Juliet?

"I always thought of Juliet as dark."

"Interesting. I love you Brits, an opinion on everything." This, from Ira, the line producer. Not a nice guy, but good with numbers.

"Any chemistry?" This from Tony, the director. He mimed an obscene gesture. "Check out the hot tub yet?"

Ira and Tony shared a laugh. I coughed.

"Actually, I had this audition."

"But you'd have liked to?" Tony was really pressing. I took this as a good sign. Glennis' casting was already set.

"Ah, sure. Absolutely. She's a bird."

"Bird?" Ira looked confused.

"Dish," I amended.

"Doll," Tony explained. "Number."

"Richmond's the executive producer," Ira volunteered. "That a problem?"

"No problem."

I got the part.

The second time I met Glennis, I was in a plaster body cast under stage lights—on set, as you may have guessed. With the heat, the glare and the body cast, I was dying, but that was in the script. Glennis offered me a shot of wheat grass.

"Freshly juiced. Right in my dressing room."

"But what is it?" Green liquid, that's what. Bright green.

"Wheat grass. It's delicious. It will perk you right up." She patted my leg.

"I'm not sure that's such a good idea."

"Oh, that's right. It's you," she said. Meaning "the prude."

"Let's pretend we never met," I offered.

It would have been easy. Except for the all-white outfit—a nurse's this time, not a shepherdess'—Glennis looked completely different. Her lovely blond hair was now Cleopatra black. She wore special contacts that rendered her sapphire eyes a violent green.

"Like me?" she asked.

"It's great. You look great. It's great." For an actor, I was pretty unconvincing.

"What?"

"The, uh, makeover."

"I think they're idiots," Glennis said. "But some pervert told them Juliet was a brunette."

I did not say "I'm the pervert." I said, "Ah, too bad." I wanted Glennis' mercy—and a drink of something besides wheat grass. I was dying of thirst.

We were working at MGM in a vintage sound stage where— *not to bother*. I certainly didn't care which Mickey Rooney/Judy Garland/Gene Kelly song-and-dance fest had once been filmed on the very premises. The air-conditioning was out, had been for hours, and no one seemed bothered but me. Tony, the director, said he *liked* the sickly sheen my skin had acquired by take number twelve. I liked it better when the sheen was faked but, *not to bother*, I was just a lowly actor and this was my big break, pun intended. My character suffered from broken ribs and a broken heart, lucky guy.

Under the sheet, the one Glennis had patted my leg through, I was stark naked. The director's bright idea. Cinema verité? My ass.

"Make you feel more vulnerable," he said.

"I'll say."

I'd like some water," I told Glennis.

"I'm not sure you are allowed."

"*What?*"

"Tony believes in realism. You know how bad hospitals are. You can ring for the nurse for hours. He wants you to feel

desperate." She patted my leg."What about acting?" I asked her.
"I'm trained to act."

"That's nice." Glennis held the wheat grass to my lips. "Tony
says I'm a natural." She nudged my lip with the tiny glass. I was too
thirsty to turn it down—

"Damn it! Damn it! What are you two doing? You weren't supposed to meet yet! There's a reason I kept you two apart." It was
Tony, the director.

Privately, I thought the reason for keeping Glennis away from
me was Richmond Egley, but no.

"I wanted to catch the thrill of your meeting on film. Glennis
says she's hot for you."

"How nice."

"He's British," Glennis explained. She patted my leg.

Richmond Egley, Glennis' boyfriend and our executive producer, let us not forget, was the object of ridicule and fascination. On the
one hand, Richmond was a record producer, only dabbling in the
business. On the other hand, he was far richer than even the studio
heads, and a genius in his field, if not theirs. The fact that he was a
music business legend and that his girlfriend was rapidly becoming
a legend in her own right caused people a certain natural confusion.

"Doesn't he know?" they would ask, meaning, "About
Glennis."

"Of course he knows."

"Doesn't he care?"

"Of course he cares."

"How does he do it, then?'

"Heroin."

That was the rumor.

While cocaine, in those days, was a socially acceptable
movie drug—there were even budgets for it built into some films—

heroin remained a horse of a different color. True, musicians did it, had always done it, but they didn't need to do much except function when they played. Richmond's heroin habit and Glennis' sex and heroin habit were the stuff of scandal. The makeup man told me that the dark green lenses were designed to disguise the fact that Glennis' sapphire eyes were clearly pinned.

The first time I heard of Richmond's heroin habit, I was getting my makeup done. It took a full two and a half hours every morning to take me from young and handsome to young and sickly to sickly and handsome. There was no hurrying a Hollywood makeup artist. Like earthquakes, they were a fact of California life, a force to be reckoned with. Like earthquakes, they could kill you.

As you'd expect, actors love to tell each other cautionary tales about makeup men—and cameramen—wreaking vengeance on a hapless star. "Be nice" is the moral of all these stories, "or you'll look like shit."

Do you know how hard it is to be nice for two and a half hours in a makeup chair? My makeup person was Val, a tall, red-haired, former chorus boy with a crush on me.

"How you doing?" Val crooned.

"Got anything for the pain? I look awful."

"Oh, good."

"I'm serious, Val. My back's killing me. The goddamn cast itches like crazy."

(Do I need to tell you Tony had me in a real body cast?)

"Try heroin," Val said. "Just a pinch."

"I couldn't do that!" There he was again, the true me, the Brit prude.

"Why not? Certain people do..."

"Who?" I gasped.

Val rolled his eyes and yanked at my hairline. Realism, schmealism. They had me in a blond wig. Go figure.

"Somebody and somebody's girlfriend."

"You're kidding."

"I thought you knew him."

"Richmond? Barely. He's great friends with a friend of mine."

"Harrison?"

Did everybody know everything? The thought made me exhausted. So did the body cast and the sleepless nights. So did the thought of dealing with Glennis and Tony and Richmond. Even with a pinch of heroin.

"He's a saint, if you ask me," Val continued. "Or closet."

"*What?*"

"Takes one to know one."

This was the first time I'd heard of Richmond's homosexuality or his heroin. I *was* shocked.

"You look stunned, darling," Val whispered.

"Just getting into character," I covered.

Every night on transatlantic phone calls, I badgered my agent. He reminded me of all the money I was making, all the exposure I'd get.

"I'll give you exposure," I snarled. "The twit had me take my knickers off. So I'd feel 'vulnerable,' he said. I'll tell you what makes me feel vulnerable—having a director who's a bloody idiot. Having a leading lady whose only real talent is for blowjobs!"

"Ah-hah!" Even across the Atlantic, I could hear my agent's sucked-in breath. "So I've heard," he said. "She's Richmond's girlfriend, isn't she?"

"Don't get your knickers in a twist. I'm just telling you the scuttlebutt. She's great at blowjobs—so I've heard."

"Ah."

You know you're in trouble when your leading lady's heroin addiction is the least of your problems. Script was another, a bigger one. The studio was screening dailies and felt the movie was depressing. I thought it was supposed to be, but what did I know? A lowly actor? A team of high-powered comedy writers had been brought in to snap up the dialogue and add a few scenes. We were getting new pages every night and delivering lines that made no sense, because the scenes they referred to hadn't been written yet, much less shot. I won't bore you with complaints about the arc of my performance, etc., etc. BUT...

"How do you stand it?" I finally asked Glennis as we finished take nineteen of a scene that had us lovingly reminiscing about the marathon race we'd met at, chatting away the last twelve miles. The writers had us separated at the finish line only to meet again at the hospital. "To an Athlete Dying Young," Glennis was to read to me. That's not depressing? Also, I have weak knees from a footballing accident.

"How do I stand it?" Glennis giggled. "Haven't you heard? I do heroin. Actually, so does Richmond. Poor Richmond, he thinks it makes him cool. It's the heartbreak of his life that he's not black. Of course, most of his acts are. Poor, poor Richmond!"

"Not what I've heard."

"Oh, that." Glennis made the fact of Richmond's fortune sound like an embarrassment. "He can't help it," she explained. "He's just plain brilliant."

That much was true. I'd added to Richmond's fortune myself by buying multiple copies of his many albums. I wore them out from sheer listening. He was that good, that *brilliant*. His eye—or ear—for what he called "the real animal" was legendary. The lousiest tape, the most damning venue, a diamond so rough it was a lump of coal to everyone else—Egley saw the gold.

Asked to explain just how it was he could pick out talent, Richmond told *Spin* magazine, "It's not so much what they are that I hear. It's what they will become." *Spin* dubbed this *potential reality.* Which was why no one could explain his being dumb enough to be with Glennis. What potential could she have? The facts, as they existed, were disaster enough.

"Do you believe in nymphomania?" Richmond asked me this that afternoon on one of his rare visits to the set.

"Is that a form of lymphoma?" I countered. Let someone else break the news.

"I suppose it is," Richmond replied, quite serious. "I think it's a form of sickness. I don't think it's a character flaw, more a way of reacting to intolerable stress, a coping device—maybe even an addiction."

We were chatting in the operating room. The new script had me having open heart surgery. I wondered what intolerable stress Glennis could be living with. I thought Richmond was rationalizing heartbreak.

"Richmond?" I interjected. "Why are you telling *me* this?"

"Glennis says you won't fuck her."

"Ah, well, yes." (Glennis was very direct, as he'd said.)

"And she says you treat her like a lady."

"I'm British, Richmond. I treat everyone like a lady."

"She says you like her."

"Ah. Actually, I do."

"I like her too."

"Richmond? Why are we having this conversation?"

"I'm giving her a house."

"That's very nice."

"I hope so. I know everyone will make fun of me for it. I know that."

"I'm sorry, Richmond."

"Me too. If I weren't so rich it would bother me, I suppose."

Abruptly, Richmond and I were laughing. You have to like a guy who can kid like that. People really do believe that money insulates you from all pain. Wrong.

"She tell you about the script changes?" I asked him.

"Of course she did. It's my money."

"What's your thought?"

"I try not to have them."

"Same here."

"This isn't my business."

"But what's your gut?"

"Oh, I think she'll be a star."

"Me too," I said. "The camera loves her."

"Well then, that makes three of us," Richmond said. "She needs friends."

Tony called for a run-through just then, and Richmond took a chair stenciled *Producer*. He was directly behind the cameraman, directly in Glennis' sight line.

"Ah, Richmond?" Tony began.

"I want him there," Glennis said. "It's my big scene."

"Imagine someone doing this to you. You're all heart," Glennis was to say to me, falling in love over the gurney, prepping me for open heart surgery.

"QUIET!" Tony shouted.

Glennis began our love scene. It was terrible. She was awful. Tony crossed to her side to give her an adjustment. Everything hinged on her grief.

"Make it real," Tony said. Behind the cameraman, Richmond cleared his throat. He held a hand to his heart. Glennis caught his eye. Their gaze held. An arc of what I might call love—or perhaps belief—flashed between them. We all felt it.

"Roll camera," Tony said. The scene unfurled.

"Imagine someone doing this to you," Glennis whispered. Grief racked her voice. The crew froze. This was *acting*. "You're all heart," she finished softly.

"Yes, yes! That's a print!" Tony shouted in stunned silence. "And cut!"

Richmond touched a hand to his eyes and walked quietly from the set.

The last time I saw Glennis was at Richmond's funeral four months later. It was the social event of the season, a full turnout of both industries. Back in town for looping, I learned the buzz on the film was very good. Buzz on Glennis was ecstatic. Hollywood loves nothing more than a new star—unless it's a tragedy.

Overdose, one story went.

HIV positive, ran another. *What are you going to do?*

Glennis, dressed now all in black, read "To an Athlete Dying Young." Grief made her radiant. Greed made her audience responsive. In addition to his controlling interest in the record company, his stock portfolio and his residuals, Richmond had left her the house in Laurel Canyon.

"You never checked out the hot tub," Glennis chided me when I crossed to the graveside to pay her my condolences.

"No," I told her.

"You never tried the wheat grass either."

"No. And I never tried the heroin."

"I *am* the heroine," Glennis said. "That's what Richmond always told me."

"He should know," I assured her.

"I think he meant spelled with an *e*."

"I'm sure he did," I lied.

As it turned out, Richmond was right. His death left Glennis so wealthy that she inherited most of his friends, her former detractors. For about six months, she phoned me regularly in London. Slowly and painfully, she was seeing through her friends.

Slowly and painfully, she was kicking her heroin addiction. I wished her well.

"Richmond said you were a True Friend," she told me through tears late one evening. "He was supposed to have an eye for the real thing."

I did what I could and Glennis did the rest.

Doomed Love enjoyed good reviews. So did Glennis. Over the next five years, to everyone's surprise, she marshaled Richmond's monies into a fortune larger still, funneling the overflow into cutting-edge AIDS research and hospice programs. Once she herself got free of her addictions, *both* of them, she was an activist herself. And quite the heroine—as Richmond always said.

Mystic Canyon

Casting Call

[LILY] An older woman, still a vision of Mary Pickford bone-china beauty. She's tough-minded, with a tender heart....LEAD (50)

MYSTIC CANYON

I know they call it the "Witch's House." To tell you the truth, that delights me. Of course, once upon a time, that wasn't true, but you get a sense of humor with age. For example, my name is Lily —of the Hollywood Hills, I joke, *not* the Valley.

I have lived in this house, high up by the Hollywood sign, for sixty-seven years. "Mystic Canyon," they call the area. If you ask me, that was Aldous' doing, putting on airs. Of course, he was a writer, and writers have a nasty habit of naming things—*the doors of perception*, for example. Why not just have the experience?

I suppose that's the actress in me. Still reluctant, after all these years, to over-think the process. "Just let it happen," my friend Jack used to say. Of course, that was easy enough for him, coming from his family, three generations of famous American actors.

"Jack, you don't have blood. You have bloodlines," I used to tease him.

"No, my darling, just lies." And then he'd exhibit that famous profile. Leave it to him to top me.

I still remember this exchange. We were standing at the big bay window in this house, the one that looks west to the ocean, or did in those days. Now it looks west into God-knows-what, a cloud of smog. Ah, Los Angeles, ah, Jack.

It was a sunny September afternoon in our barely perceptible fall. Jack was making a slow exit from our lives. I was having trouble with the curtain.

"You look sad," Jack said.

"I am sad. All of this"—I gestured to our little group of friends, Jack, Aldous, Maria and Erich, my husband—"is ending."

"Don't be so dramatic."

"Me? Jack, you *define* dramatic."

He turned up his glorious nose at this remark. Jack could protest, but I knew and I was beginning to know that I knew. Funny, *psychic* comes from the word *psyche*, for *soul*, so we all have the gift in some form, but it sure makes people uncomfortable—myself included at the beginning.

It started one full-moon night, a few weeks later, when all of us were picnicking up where they put the observatory. We were talking about clairvoyance. What nowadays they call ESP. While the moon shifted in and out between the clouds, Aldous regaled us all with tales of the British spiritualists. Their antics. Their high jinks. Their high spirits, you could say. A man named Alan Ford was touring the country at the time. Ford was a medium of great report. Aldous knew him personally and spoke of him, I thought, with just a touch of envy.

"The spirit world? No matter what he says, I don't know and I don't want to know," Jack sniffed. "Let them surprise me as I shall certainly surprise them!"

"They mention spiritual gifts in the Bible," Maria put in mildly.

"Bosh," Jack said. "Live in the moment or we're dead."

"Eventually," Aldous observed. "As we understand it. It's been argued—by me, of course—that *this* is the death."

"Bosh," Jack repeated. "Look. There's Orion."

He pointed a bony finger up between the clouds. I followed it to the constellation, clearly visible—not like today—at his fingertip. Suddenly, instead of the starlit night, I saw Jack himself—stretched out, hands folded, dressed for the grave. A calla lily lay beside him.

"Don't leave us," I blurted out.

"Are you all right?" Maria asked.

"She's just blathering," Jack said.

"What is it?" Aldous wanted to know. He would.

"Oh," I fumbled. "I just love it when all of us are together." I wasn't about to tell Jack or Aldous what I'd seen.

At the moment, Jack, very much alive, was pointing out Sagittarius, the archer. "I love the stars," Jack said. "They draw us to size."

"Easy for you to say. You are one," I ribbed him.

"And you an actor's actor," Jack told me. I have cherished that remark.

Do I need to tell you Jack's funeral was a photograph of what I'd seen that night? Do I need to tell you this fact made me crazy? I told Erich, "I saw Jack lying dead. The night we had that picnic. I should have told him."

"How could you?" Erich asked. "You hadn't even told me. And you generally tell me everything—don't you?"

After that, gingerly, I began admitting to what I saw. Not to just anybody, mind you, but to Erich. We both agreed to keep it just between the two of us. After all, I was a working actress and I couldn't afford any brouhaha. Who would want a psychic on his set? No director I knew. They were supposed to be the all-knowing ones. And so, no matter what I saw, Erich was the only one I told. No, that's not quite true. I also told my journal.

I recorded earthquakes, forest fires, rumblings of war. Before he rose to power, I saw Hitler clearly. *A little man who looks like Charlie Chaplin but with a mustache*, I wrote. Over time, I became both comfortable and uncomfortable with my perceptions. I grew accustomed to their accuracy as well.

"Are they warnings?" I wondered to Erich. "Am I meant to act on them?" This question pressed on me increasingly.

"What would a warning do but create pain or panic?" Erich asked. "And isn't destiny *destiny*?"

He was right. There was destiny to be reckoned with and not by someone as puny as me—a bit player, not a star.

The visions became clearer, less alarming, more frequent. I began to be able to discern not only major dramatic turns of events but small, less seismic ones. Often, they bore happy tidings. Was good news any less a burden than bad? Could I share it without disturbing some delicate mechanism? Frankly, I didn't know—sometimes, it was just too hard to hold it in.

"I see you having the most beautiful children!" I might burst out to a pair of newlyweds, never including suspicious detail.

"I'm sure you'll do brilliantly," I might encourage a wavering ingenue, deleting mention of her heady successes, clear as headlines in my mind's eye.

"The picture will be gigantic," I told my neighbor, the beleaguered camera operator on Selznick's epic *Gone With the Wind*.

"What a future you'll have!" I told the young George Cukor, who was never as secure as he always let on.

Meanwhile, my own career took its long and winding path. Like Erich's and my love, it seemed to have a happy life of its own, unfolding gently and continually against the odds. My hair silvered. My waist thickened. My resumé grew and so did my skills. I became what Jack had told me I was, "an actor's actor." Call me a bit player, call me a character actress, I could and would deliver the small pieces of business that rounded out a memorable scene.

Cukor, Sturges, Capra. I worked with the greats, the near-greats, the once-greats. I saw them come and I saw them go. Sometimes twice, if you believe my journal. I worked constantly and very happily. The camera liked me and so did my directors.

"Of course they do," Erich would brag, stroking my cheek. "It's your skin."

I am blessed with perfect skin, an English complexion, that even at my age is still roses and cream, very soft and delicate. Erich, the cinematographer on one of my films, fell in love with the way his lights caught my skin—or vice versa. He proposed to me on wrap night. I accepted and we eloped—all the way to Santa Barbara!

Although I didn't know what to make of it then, I saw, quite distinctly, on my wedding night, the tumor Erich would one day hide from the studio, the doctor and even himself. It appeared to me as a dark and terrible blot beneath his heart. At first, I took it for sorrow—Erich's first wife had died young, leaving him to come to this country a brokenhearted young widower until he met me.

Later I knew the sorrow was mine; the tumor was Erich's. The journal records it all with terrible clarity: the growing shadows, my dire hints, Erich's stubborn refusal to see a doctor, my badgering, Erich's balkiness, my final blurting out of the reason for my concern—too late. God, how I loved that man! What fun he was! This house, this wonderful house, was his bequest to me when he passed on. Some days I still feel we live together.

It was Erich himself, fading, who urged me to break my rule of silence. "Never mind about destiny," he told me. "You could help people."

"Maybe. Maybe not. You wouldn't see a doctor. I did tell you."

"I'm stubborn. All cinematographers are. We want things to look the way we see they can look in our mind's eye. Anything that doesn't fit our vision, we just keep out of frame."

"I think you're right about that," I laughed. "And I'm just the opposite. Things I don't want to see are always intruding."

"Makes us a match."

In a sense, Erich's death left me both secure and with nothing to lose. I'd had my career. I'd had my great love. What did I need with people's good opinion?

I'd told my journal about Fatty's troubles in San Francisco. I confided my concerns about Jean. I told myself it was an experiment, that I was writing down impressions, nothing more, but I found myself unable not to act on them....

"Trains are lovely, don't you think? Why fly when you could have that lovely trip through the desert?" I dropped a hint to

Carole that went blithely ignored. She was a lovely woman, hurrying into life—and into death, with that terrible crash.

"Be careful," I advised Monty. "If you go more slowly in life, you can enjoy the view." He was not going slowly that night up on Mulholland. He wasn't watching the view or the curves.

"Don't drink so much," I told an anxious Marilyn. She was always so worried she was never good enough, not a "real" actress, like the rest of us—whatever that meant. "Don't do it with the pills." She took me for a meddlesome biddy, but she was sweet about it, just disinterested in what I had to say.

As far as these beloved darlings went, I altered no one's destiny. As long as they wouldn't—or couldn't—listen, my previews left me powerless. Who knows? For all their sweetness, maybe as stars they were too high up to hear things from a bit player like me.

That's when I turned to counseling—at psychic fairs, the kind rife with charlatans and True Believers. Holding the hand of eager aspirants from Ohio or Georgia, I encouraged their dreams, told them the good I saw, the paths with rewards in sight—at least to me.

Occasionally, they listened. That was rewarding for me. I felt I had been of service. Not to make it sound so glum, I truly enjoyed it—that lovely young actress with the broken heart, the one I guided into singing again? I don't know if she would have thought of it on her own without me. Of course, I remember to credit her sister too. She brought her to me. What a funny little button! A policewoman! We met when the house was broken into the second time. She reminded me of a feisty little terrier, like Asta from *The Thin Man*.

About this time, I took up gardening.

My house crowns a small hill laced with gravel paths. Between them, I planted cacti, desert-blooming plants, hybrids adapted to our sandy, arid soil. Working my paths, I came to know what had now become a neighborhood. Houses had grown up at the foot of my hill, houses filled with children. My garden brought hummingbirds. The birds brought children, and the children brought me their dreams. How I wished Erich were here to share them.

"Yes! You can do that!" I encouraged them.

"You'll see. You'll do well on that test Tuesday. Just remember to read about coal mines."

Last Thursday, pausing in my garden, I saw myself quite clearly, resting peacefully in a small chapel amid stephanotis and calla lilies; I saw Erich hovering, looking exactly as he did on our wedding night, like he couldn't wait to get the formalities over with!

Dear Erich! Waiting patiently for me so many years.

In the vision, I had a small, visible bruise on my right temple. Even the coroner's makeup didn't cover it. A fall? Another break-in? Destiny is destiny. I wasn't given those details, just the happy ending I assume, opening this door, that in the long view the details scarcely matter.

WILLIE

Casting Call

[THE DIRECTOR] Our director is well bred, well spoken and well thought of—just ask him. He's worldly and world-weary, in part because he's part of it....LEAD (58)

WILLIE

When I first met Willow Brooks, she was twenty years old and looked thirty—old enough to know better and young enough to enjoy doing it anyway. She was, in life as on screen, a blonde of the kind men dream about. Speaking for myself, my dreams of Willow began as romantic idylls—Willie with windblown hair, romping on a dune above Malibu—and ended as nightmares. Willie on locked ward reciting her script as if the person who shot holes in it was a cameraman and not a petty mobster.

Willie was one of those blondes whose face held no shadows. The planes of her cheeks, the curve of her earlobe, the line of her neck, her shoulder, her arm, her—it was all molded light. Off screen, as on, she was a goddess, and most men I knew, certainly myself, became True Believers very quickly.

The day I met Willie, she stole my parking place at the lot. This was no small matter, even back then. As always, I was running late , and I turned into the lot with the same velocity I'd taken the turns on Beverly Glen to get there. I was late for a studio meeting, slicking back my hair as I nosed down a row toward my slot and—*bam.* She was backing out of my space in a vintage Ferrari. Do I have to tell you how much I loved the car, the one it would cost me three thousand dollars to repair? Not my car, hers. Willie was very per-suasive—tears, desperate remorse—and what man can resist a wounded Ferrari, which is the image I used for Willie herself that first time when I cast her.

"The girl is beautiful but she's been treated badly, bashed around a little. You want to help her out, fix her up—like a mis-treated Ferrari. I know you know what I mean." The men around the teak table knew what I meant. "I'm thinking Willow Brooks."

"Willow...Brooks?" She was not yet a household name, not yet a fixture in the clubs, not yet the golden apple of everyone's eye.

"Terrible name."

"It's real."

"Mmm."

"So's the hair. So's everything else."

I took out the studio shots I had prepared for the occasion. Hurrell was not only a friend but also a neighbor, and he had done the work for me with only the smallest of chuckles as I signed his considerable check. (I wanted to keep him as a friend, you see.)

The shots were perfect, and most perfect in relation to the role I was casting. Willie wore an expression of both openness and containment. This was a woman with a secret. The shots posed a question in the heart of every man who saw them: Can I have her?

What's her training? What's her background? What does it matter? I made my sale.

The less said about Willie's training and background the better—even now. The point was, as it always is, that the camera loved her. I have heard a producer say that he thinks the camera catches every molecule on a set, not merely what is visible to the lens. If that's true, looking at Willie, the camera captured desire. And not merely mine—that of every man who saw her—grip, cameraman, best boy.

We were in the second week of shooting when she moved in with me. I was separated from my second wife—she'd become a nasty drunk, too fond of clubs and too eager for the columns—so I was conveniently alone when the phone rang at two A.M. and Willow begged me to let her come over.

A director is a complicated thing to his stars: father, lover, priest, protector. You have to know when to be what. I knew from the first syllable that Willie needed to come to me, that this was something more than midnight jitters and I had better act.

She arrived at my bungalow at the Beverly Hills—the wife kept the house—wrapped in a man's bathrobe and a waxen pallor.

"I think I killed him," she said.

"Who?"

"My boyfriend."

This was the first I'd heard of any boyfriend, but, then, an actress is many things to her director: mistress, muse, child, simple clay, the medium for his desires, the vessel for his fantasies. You've heard it before and all of it is true.

"Sit down."

I offered her a chair and a shot of brandy. She reached for the bottle instead. Two long slugs and she could focus. She handed the bottle back, unlike my wife. I was looking at the robe. Silk and very expensive, Sulka probably, monogrammed. The initials belonged to a famous gangster and so, evidently, did she.

"Yes," she answered. "I'm sorry. I wanted the job. He got the script for me."

As I've said, an actress's relation to her director is a complicated thing, and while I had never approached her, never would during filming, Willie had allowed me to believe she was both unattached and interested. I was both of those things. Like any director, I love a good story. Not that she was telling it.

"Dead?" I asked.

"It was his gun," she answered.

"Prints? Witnesses?" (Forget about motive.)

"I was wearing gloves." She took them from the pocket of the robe and handed them to me. One of them was slightly splattered with what I took to be blood—stage blood looks so much more real. I pocketed the gloves.

"Let me run you a bath."

"Thanks." She let the robe drop and followed me into the bathroom.

As I've said, a director's relationship to his actress is

very complicated. Her gesture might have been seductive, but I read it as a child's blind faith. Like a faithful daddy, I ran her a tub, looked past her nakedness, left her to soak in a nectar of hot oils and water and retreated to think in the chair where she'd left her robe.

Outside the window, the sun was rising. Already! Why didn't I call the police? you might be wondering. Well, I would have, but I had a film to make and we—Willow and I and the small army I generaled—had a six A.M. call. I phoned my driver instead.

"Pick me up in fifteen minutes," I told him. "Stop for coffee and a quart of orange juice. Get some sherbet too, if you can."

I am a dapper man, and by the time Willie appeared in the bathroom doorway, I had assembled a creditable wardrobe for her —a pair of good gabardine pants, a fine cotton shirt from Turnbull & Asser, a lizard belt she could loop at the waist, a pair of loafers, a fine tweed jacket. The effect was dashing and declared to the world that we were lovers. So what? I was separated, and stranger things have happened in Hollywood than an outset romance between a director and his beautiful star.

Willie dressed quickly and quietly. I handed her a brush to run through her hair. My bungalow had a fireplace with a pre-laid fire. I doused it with lighter fluid, lit a match, added the robe and the spattered gloves. Willie and I watched them burn. By the time my driver arrived, we had the sleepy, nerved-up energy of new lovers announcing their involvement to the world.

Judging by the papers, the police made short work of the crime scene. An inside job, they declared it—and it was. As with many mob murders, the law performed only the most pro forma investigation: *Let them work it out* was the unspoken rationale.

By that time, I knew a great deal more about Willie. For example, "It was on purpose. The car accident, I mean."

"You planned it?" I looked at Willie's guileless blue eyes. So I was the sucker! I gave her my fondest smile.

"I wanted to meet you. I'd read the script, like I told you."

All studios have their ties to the mob. There is something about money and power and sex. They act as vectors and steer the most legitimate people to the darkest intersections. So she'd seen the script. The boyfriend had gotten it for her, and the less I knew about how, the better. She was doing a wonderful job—and she wasn't a bad housemate either.

I believe I am like most directors in that I will go to almost any length to make a good film. In this case, the lengths were my Bel-Air home, profits on several films, some choice acreage in what is now Encino. My presumed involvement with Willie did not escape the attention of the columnists nor of my estranged wife and her attorneys. Willie's work was everything I'd hoped and worth the price.

We made three films together. They form the cornerstone of my middle career and the arc of Willie's rising star. Our marriage was somewhat less successful, but I am not quibbling. We got along better than many a husband and wife, and it genuinely grieved me when I had to divorce her. If a director's relationship with his actress is a complicated thing, his relationship to his wife is even more so.

"But why?" Willie asked me, forgetting that the basis of our successful life was unasked questions. I did not tell her that I saw her need for me was finished. I did not tell her that I felt I had served her to the extent of my capacities, that like her gangster boyfriend, my usefulness to her was at an end. Let her figure that out later. I would step aside before I became an impediment. That was my thinking. I am a director and I was directing, that's all. My script called for an amicable parting of the ways. There were other actresses I was interested in working with. She'd find other directors....That was my script.

I was as surprised as anyone—no, more surprised—to discover that Willie did not embrace her new freedom with the eagerness I had mistakenly seen in her. The studio loaned her out to a new director and a fine one. I agreed with the maneuver, believing it would serve both of us to move on—at least in our work. As I explained it to Willie, we both needed to work with others for the sake of our craft. The personal decision was a painful but pragmatic one. I was the keeper of her secrets and now expendable. My safety required I give her free egress—or so I believed.

It took her all of six months to wind up dead. Locked ward preceded it, a studio decision.

What did they want me to do about that? I wondered. We were divorced. It was her new director's problem. I didn't return the calls. Delusions, they said. Some talk about shooting someone or being shot. Like a B movie, some fantasy about gangsters and running for her life. In this fantasy, I was cast as her savior.

In the years of our life together, I had somehow forgotten the moment when she first doffed her robe and presented herself to me naked, trusting as a child. I had forgotten that I was her father, priest and protector as well as her lover. I had forgotten. I was merely protecting myself. I did not mean to hurt her.

What I remembered was the initial accident she planned for me. I don't believe that I planned hers. I have asked myself that. But that is a different story, mine, and this was hers.

They found her in the bedroom, alone, wearing a man's bathrobe, mine. A heart attack, they said. At her age? An accident involving malnutrition, nerves, drugs perhaps—it was never very clear. The circumstances were as shady as her past.

I did not mean to cut her adrift. I did not mean to leave her victim to her darker impulses. I did not even remember that she was first of all my child and not my spouse. As I have said, a director's relationship to his actress is a delicate thing. Willie came to me asking to be protected and I protected her—of course I also protected my film. "Our" film, you could say. And even in the end, I was only protecting our careers.

Number Six

Casting Call

[STAR REPORTER] A Pouilly-Fuissé blonde. She's clear, she's chill, and she's chilling....LEAD (66) POSSIBLE NUDITY.

NUMBER SIX

⌒⌒

"In the end, I don't think I'm the reason I couldn't keep them. Wives, I mean." The director licked salt from the edge of his margarita, eyeing me over the rim. "It's not easy in America. We've got this obsession with celebrities—and I am one."

He certainly was. Tall as a steeple, with a face as grandly ravaged as a bombed cathedral, he was gaunt as Abe Lincoln and blessed with a photogenic shock of snow-white hair. You would recognize him. A dyed-in-the-wool, certified-by-the-tabloids celebrity—the kind who was snapped at openings with his progressively younger dates on his arm. I mentioned this.

"Actually, they're not getting younger. I'm getting older." He had a point. I noted that I—late thirties and counting—felt young and pretty beside him. My years of distinguished reporting dissolved in the heat of his masculine charisma. Who says actors are the knockouts? It's the directors who have the voltage. Trust me on that. They have to have it. It is their *job* to get people to do what they want—like marry them.

This interview was taking place in a back booth at the Sherry Netherland. It was once, in the late seventies, very much a movie hotel and was now much less so. My director—see what I mean?—stubbornly clung to his preferred hotel, his preferred bar, his preferred booth. It was the catbird booth, where he could eye the door and all who entered could spot him and know they had arrived. He returned to the subject of his many wives. I had the distinct impression he was directing our interview. As a reporter, I'd felt that way before, but usually with CIA helmsmen or Arab potentates.

"I was saying, I'm a celebrity and some of my wives—

my ex-wives—may have started out that way but it doesn't last long. In a sense, being a wife becomes their celebrity—no matter how they started out. I don't know if you remember this but Johnna, my fourth wife, was actually quite a talented actress. In fact, that's how we met. As we envisioned it, we'd have this long and wonderful collaboration. We liked working together. Of course, we both got wonderful reviews—until she married me."

"Then what happened?"

I was remembering the divorce, not the marriage. He'd dumped her, very publicly, for another actress, whom he also married.

"Something very strange. Now, before people knew we were together, they thought this girl was very talented. I'm telling you, she got great reviews, and not just in my movies. Then, and this was hard for us, we tied the knot and her luck turned. Suddenly people began to wonder if I was casting her *because* she was my wife. They began to say maybe I should try casting someone else. Now, to my eye—and I do think I know acting—her performances were still wonderful, but the critics sure didn't think so. They found some very mysterious faults."

"They were stingy," I chimed in.

"Maybe so."

Even after two hours of tape and several steep drinks, he was cagey about the critics. No wonder he had survived four decades of filmmaking and three of world-class celebrity.

"I'll tell you a funny thing. It's not something I like to admit, but I began to wonder if they were right. I started urging the girl to work with other directors—some of our friends maybe. Before I married her, they all thought she was grand. Once we tied the knot, her offers dried up. I remember what she used to say: 'It's like they think I'm a double agent or something.'"

Across the room a flashbulb snapped. Reflexively the director leaned toward me and flashed a winning smile. I took this as a compliment. I must have looked as young and pretty as I felt with this old grizzled lion. The bulb flashed again and yet again before the maître d' intervened.

"Let them have their fun," the director said when the maître d' crossed to our table to apologize. "I'm in good company."

Moments later, the maître d' sent us a bottle of Veuve Clicquot to compensate for our embarrassment. Who was embarrassed? It was my favorite champagne—not Dom Perignon, not Perrier-Jouët, not Taittinger—or I might have been more careful.

"To writers," the director toasted. "Where would I be without them?"

"How refreshing," I said dryly. "Are you speaking as a director or a celebrity?"

"Tsk-tsk, you are a suspicious young thing."

Young thing. That was blatant flattery. No wonder they'd all married him. Even after Willow Brooks.

"You were in the middle of a story," I reminded him. "About number three or four. The one right after Willow Brooks."

"Oh, yes, Willie," he sighed. A ghost stalked his long, bony face. "Poor Willie and now poor Johnna."

"She's working again," I reminded him. "All the time."

"Her suicide attempt was the best press she'd had in years."

"And unlike Willow Brooks she lived to tell the tale."

"Her version." He fingered the salt on his glass.

"Yours?"

"I never abandoned her. The critics did."

"Really."

"I hate America," he replied. It wasn't the non sequitur it seemed. "It's so parochial. They couldn't let us have our fun. Celebrities are like politicians, dependent on their constituency's goodwill. Celebrity wives are like political wives. They're supposed to be 'the little woman.' God forbid they *think*. Any signs of independence and the media takes them to task. The American media is so cynical. They simply can't conceive of two talented people married to each other. Somebody has to be using somebody. Somebody has to be a no-talent or climber to keep their equation right."

"What do you suppose it is?" I asked.

"Envy." He said it like a coroner declaring the body "dead." Who could argue?

"In America, you're only allowed to have so much. Johnna could have me or her talent. Unfortunately, she loved me. I really think she hung in a little too long for her own good."

The ghost walked again. This time I was certain the grief was genuine. It touched me—then I remembered the details.

"Wait a minute. You left her, didn't you?"

"Yes, I'm afraid I did. She was very depressed. I was rather callow, sad to say." A sickle of smile creased his face.

"I don't believe that version," I told him.

"What do you mean?" he protested, genuinely shocked.

Now, I am very good at my job, reporting. And, perhaps because I started out in crime, moving on from crime to politics, if you think there's a difference, I have learned to trust my gut. I didn't know what I meant, but I did know I was right. I pressed. "You're still in love with her, aren't you?"

Yes was the answer if you asked me.

"I'm still in love with all of them," he said mournfully. "They were great girls, all of them. I miss something about each of them. And I'm glad they've been able to go on to better things. I like to think I was a little help to them at a certain point in their careers. But then, it was just too much, being married to me. Nobody saw them anymore. They were invisible. They began to fade. What else could I do but cut them loose?"

"To deception," I toasted.

"Self-deception?" he asked. "You're looking at me like I'm Jack the Ripper."

"This is the best rationale for womanizing I have ever heard." Was the champagne talking? "You didn't tire of them and move on. They grew tiresome from the burden of being with you. You didn't screw them over. You gave them their freedom. It's charming."

"Not tiresome. Tired. They were never tiresome. They were women."

"How chivalrous."

"I'm glad you give me some credit. For a while there you were looking at me like I was Dracula, sucking the blood and talent out of a succession of sweet young things. They, the media, just wouldn't let us continue."

"I met your fifth wife," I told him. "She wasn't so sweet."

"Ah. My doing, actually." This post facto chivalry was wearing on me. Or maybe the champagne was making me quarrelsome.

"C'mon. She was difficult," I told him. "I'm sure she was difficult before she met you. In fact, I met her before she met you. I wrote about her for *The Times* on her breakthrough picture. The one where she played the gangster's wife. Before she had her accent removed."

"I always liked the accent. She used to use it at home."

I was remembering the tabloid stories of their on-set romance, the way it jettisoned both of them up a level. Their subsequent marriage had been short and, to my eye, very serviceable. Her association with him had lent her credibility. His with her had revived his fading reputation and allowed him to mourn her departure publicly—as if it hadn't been planned.

"You don't have to believe me," the director said, "but America has a quota system. You are allowed only so much success before they want you to pay for it. Haven't you ever noticed how the long-term celebrities—the lifers, I call them—have always got their compensatory crosses to bear? Liz Taylor and her operations and addictions. Cher and her bad luck with men. Where would they be without them? It's all soap opera. They get the public addicted to their story line. It's even true for me. The public makes as much of my women as it does of my work."

"I'm hungry," I told him. "And you haven't talked about your work at all. We've done three hours of tape and it's all tabloid stuff."

"Sweetheart, I *am* tabloid stuff," the director chided me. "And how can I separate my wives from my work? After all, I worked with all of them."

This much was true. Always before—and always briefly after marrying them—he had worked with his wives. They had given him indelible work. His canon was built on the complicated, glowing performances he elicited from women. He poured me another glass of champagne. He signaled for the check.

"We'll eat in my suite," he said. "That way, we can talk about the work with a little privacy."

I dimly remember feeling a sense of alarm.

The director's suite at the Sherry was on the 22nd floor, on the park side, of course. From the street, you could spot it because it had a sort of bird's nest, a small, windowed room jutting out from the rest of the building. From the bird's nest, Central Park spread before you like a bas-relief map, the kind children make for geography class. We were standing at a window, looking down.

"The film opens here, of course," the director said. "The lovers are walking below." He pointed down toward the children's zoo, where lovers were, indeed, walking. The director put his hand on the back of my neck, directing my attention.

I joined the game. "Yes, and it closes here too. We pull back, up and away."

"To this room. Where the lovers are talking—talking about their former selves. The way it started, I see them as old—he grizzled but she softly glowing like that Yeats poem."

A little bell went off in me as we improvised this scenario.

In fact, a big bell went off in me, but I ignored it. After all, food had been ordered. It would arrive any moment and we were, finally, talking about his work—or were we?

"I cheated on Johnna to give her her freedom."

"What a line. Do you believe that?"

"Oh, yes," he assured me solemnly. "Our marriage was killing her. It was killing her career, which amounted to the same thing."

"Not for all of us," I told him.

"Really?" Even through the champagne, I could see him looking at me with genuine interest, wondering if anyone, really, could separate "self" from "career."

"The flirtation with...with wife number five, as you call her, was an affront that I knew Johnna could not tolerate. She considered her vulgar—and she was—but charming."

I remembered the ghastly tabloid shots of Johnna stricken and drawn, always juxtaposed with the shots of her smiling husband and his new lover. This had been for her own good?

"Let's talk about what you want to do next," I suggested, struggling for higher ground.

"That sounds like a direction," he chided.

"What *do* you want to do next?"

"I thought dinner with you and then a nice, long conversation."

"About work." I was trying to set guidelines.

"Work? All right. Yours and mine. More champagne?"

I could never explain it to my editor Sam's satisfaction—or mine either, I suppose. It wasn't a fluff piece, exactly. It was too biting for that, but it did make the man out to be fascinating, charismatic, brilliant, etc., etc., etc. The piece, and the director, were the talk of the cocktail circuit. In my own literary circles, there was fascinated shock that I, the tigress, seemed to have succumbed to him. Not to Kissinger. Not to Kennedy. To him.

A movie director.

Sam said it best—or at least loudest. He exploded at me in the editorial offices overlooking Fifth Avenue but not my obvious weaknesses.

"You would think you were a sitting duck and not the famed 'author of three volumes of political essays!'" Volume rising. "You were sent to interview this director to unlock the *political* secrets of his success. You made him sound...*SEXY!*"

Now, there's a slur.

"He was charming," I managed weakly. My editor glared.

"Charming? There's a limp word."

"He was not limp," I volunteered, teasing.

"Are you telling me you were a victim of testosterone poisoning?"

"Maybe."

"You wrote an entire piece about how he fucked women and how his fucking them and fucking them over later was good for them. You made him sound like some kind of sexual Pygmalion."

"I quoted him, Sam. I didn't say I believed it."

Sam fumed, using words that made him sound like an outraged librarian. "I admit, the piece was well liked. All right, very well liked. But I expected something different from you."

"Oh, Sam," I said. "I'm sorry I let you down. I'm sorry I wrote a piece about sex instead of sexual politics."

I was thinking, oh, Sam, no wonder I never slept with you. What woman could sleep with a man who expected something different from her, as if the usual, her female self, weren't enough?

"Is it true you've been offered a contract by THEM?" Sam screamed this as if I'd just gone over to the Nazis.

"Why, Sam!" Deny, deny, deny—a mobster had given me that advice years ago.

"Is it true?"

What the hell, I wasn't a mobster. Why deny anything?

"Actually, two of them."

It was true. The first was a contract to write for "them"—a very slick magazine that specialized in celebrities and power politics. The second was a contract, from a very good house, to write the director's biography. This contract came with an overwhelming advance attached to it. Even though there were rumors that the director was now attached to me—or vice versa.

As usual, the rumors were true. You get the picture.

INT. SUITE—EARLY MORNING
Two lovers lie in bed, enjoying a leisurely breakfast.
ME
I can't accept this contract.
I'd be compromised.

DIRECTOR
(grinning raffishly)
Of course you will.
A little compromise will be good for you.

He was right. And that was eleven years ago. When the biography came out, they called it *An* Intimate *Biography*, simple as that. It sold like popcorn. And made both of us more famous. Can anyone really separate "self" from "career"?

I'm number six.

DIAMOND HEART

Casting Call

[MARGARET] An agent, not a writer, but she might call herself the paperback edition of Dorothy Parker. Not quite the real thing, but close enough....LEAD (76)

DIAMOND HEART

"I'm willing," I told her, "to work things through." This was a lie. I was willing to ruin her and it would take me a little more time.

I'm a literary agent—a dying species, if you ask me. I'm in it for quality, not quantity, and I make that clear to my clients. I represent eighteen writers, ten of them dead. Several of my dead writers have done very well with me. Sales to movies have made for some comfortable survivors, not that the films have been all my writers might have hoped.

It was a movie sale that first set me and Judith to squabbling. Judith and I had a lot to squabble over. Both of us had invested a great deal in our relationship. When I took her on, Judith was a wanna-be writer. She'd sent me her manuscript and a—the only word is pathetic—letter, nine pages long, explaining why I should read over typos, bad punctuation, faded typing ribbons. *Just read it*, the letter pleaded. *Then tell me what you think.*

Well, I did read it—despite typos, a loose comma hand and an array of type styles. Something in the letter had caught my attention and I read on, out of charity more than hope, I think.

That was the beginning, and the beginning paid for my midtown town house, not to mention what it did for Judith.

"Of course, I'll need to have this properly typed," I told her. "And I may need to go over it with a two-and-a-half pencil."

"Edit me?" Judith yelped. As if she were Proust.

"Just touch it up grammatically," I soothed her.

I did that, paid for the typing out of my own pocket, took a pencil and a fine-tooth comb to the manuscript, before I sent it anywhere. What can I tell you? I knew gold when I saw it.

"I need money," Judith told me. "Can you hurry things up a little bit?"

I loaned her money from my own pocket. Before you think I'm a philanthropist, let me tell you, the manuscript was that good. It was only a question of when, not if, it would sell. I'm talking about *Diamond Heart*, of course. Judith wrote it in Laundromats and on her breaks at the coffee shop. When she said "Things are a little tight," she meant food stamps. Judith was one tough cookie, even then—twins, a husband on drugs, and still she found time to write.

"I just do it fast, that's all," she explained to me. I thought then of asking her to publish under a pseudonym. *Diamond Heart* had an unmistakable authenticity, the silver-spoon, born-to-the-manner, insider's take on the world of the upper crust. I didn't want Judith on food stamps surfacing in *People* magazine.

"But I'm a great story!" Judith wailed when I told her my desire she use a pseudonym. "Rags to riches."

"Trust me on this one," I counseled. "Forget rags to riches. Forget little Judy Kronske of Laundromat and food stamp fame. Choose your future."

"I like my name," she protested.

"How can anyone like your name?" I asked. (Her name was Judy, after all. At least she didn't spell it with an *i*.)

"Judith," she replied.

"And the last name? Kronske has a certain—" I paused tactfully.

"Plebeian air?" Judith nailed it.

"Yes."

"I'll use Muir."

"Muir?"

"It's my final offer."

"Judith Muir. All right. Not bad."

Diamond Heart by Judith Muir sold twenty million copies,

nine hundred thousand in hardcover. I'd say it was a publishing phenomenon, but she followed *Diamond Heart* with *Emerald Eyes* and that with *Sapphire Soul*. I added a country house to my town house and then a condo in Bermuda. Judith, sad to say, stayed Judy Kronske in her soul.

With her monies from *Diamond Heart*, she put her husband, Phil, through detox and bought a mansion—a mansion?—outside Omaha, Nebraska. The *Emerald* dollars paid for an art tour of Europe—plus a five-hundred-acre farm, also outside of Omaha. By the time *Sapphire* was in the stores, she'd donated a library to the Omaha County Community College and bought a Dodge Ram pickup. I mention all of this so you understand the seeds of our conflict had fertile ground.

I wouldn't say I like my authors dead—that sounds terrible—but I find the living ones can drive me a little crazy. I was handling Judith's career nicely, if you ask me. And I did get asked, frequently, because Judith, at my suggestion, had a "no press" policy. Combine a best-seller with an insistence on anonymity and you had the makings of some good publicity. And what would Judith want to talk about? Her children's 4-H projects? No, better she leave the press to me.

The Judith I invented, the one I presented to the press, was a romantic recluse. Her dazzling novels, steeped in historic detail, were the product of her travels and superb education. All right, so I was doing a little writing of my own. The fictional Judith didn't have a husband from Archie Bunker's gene pool or twins—Jimmy and Timmy—with twin behavioral disorders that wrought havoc on her time, attention and productivity. The year Jimmy got into trouble with drugs, Timmy got in trouble with sex. It was an act of God that gave his girlfriend a spontaneous abortion and his mother a novelette—*Ruby Throat*—that outsold all her other books, even slim and overpriced as it was.

"I want my life back," the squabble began. I had sold theatrical rights for *Ruby Throat* to the highest bidder, not a director little Judy Kronske respected. Her life back? This struck me as thankless. Judith's novelette had just rated a piece in *The Times Book Review*, favorable. A sidebar quoted me on the writing habits of the "elusive author." I gave her a laptop and a habit of cruises for final drafts. What was I going to say? "Oh, she seems to type them out between family counseling sessions and worrying about her husband Phil's philandering?"

"Yes!" Judith said. "Or let me say it."

"You?" I admit, I was astonished. I thought Judy Kronske was lucky to have me and knew it. I like my writers either dead or grateful, but you would too if you'd walked in my shoes.

Speaking of which, Judith bought hers at Payless. I bought mine at Cole Haan. I wear a size 4, plaid pleated Presbyterian skirts and Laura Ashley blouses. Before you think *yuppie*, think William Hamilton's *New Yorker* cartoons. I am the nervous, well-bred young woman who talks earnestly of literature and how to best present escargot.

"I want my life back," Judith said. "I've earned it."

"Judith, Judith! You always tell me you love your life."

"I do."

(How could she? Jimmy was into alcohol now and Timmy had a new girlfriend, black, who shot drugs. I heard all of this on the phone. I never *saw* Judith. She thought New York was "scary.")

"Well, then, leave it alone."

"You leave it alone. Stop inventing me. I read what you said in *The Times*. It isn't true."

"They don't want *truth*, Judith."

"By 'they' I assume you mean my fans?"

"Yes. I hate that word. Can't you say 'readers'?

"My 'readers,' then. How would you know what they want?"

"Wait a minute, Judith." Did I sound a little cross?

"Judy."

"I found you. You wrote me this pathetic letter and I took pity on you." Did I sound condescending?

"I wrote a best-seller, Margaret."

"Technically."

"Oh, I get it." Judith was using her Judy Kronske voice, one nasty little whine.

"Judith?"

Silence.

"Judy?"

"Yeah?"

I was in over my head and I knew it. Why hadn't I seen it coming? Usually, my client instincts were excellent. Or were they? As I've said, half my list is dead. Suddenly Judith and I were in this huge squabble. And she was half my income!

"Could we meet to talk this over?" I meant metaphorically.

"Where?" Judy Kronske could nail a thing down.

"I'll meet you halfway, Judith."

"Where's that? Toledo?" Judith gave her Kronske giggle, a nasty little sound she herself usually edited.

"Please, Judy. I hate to fight."

"But you like to win, don't you?"

Judith and I met at the Russian Tea Room. She flew in from Omaha. (Phil had given up drugs, taken up flying and bought a plane.) I asked for a bad table. My usual was too public. I got there early to get my ducks in a row. "A simple change in strategy," I planned to tell her, little Judy Kronske, the housewife who got lucky, if you ask me.

"Margaret?"

I hadn't recognized her.

"Judy?"

When had she grown so soignée? When had my own clothes stratagem—the girls' school look—grown so dated on me, seemed so jejune? Little Judy Kronske was wearing a simple Escada day suit and a chilly smile. She was not wearing the extra thirty pounds she always told me about. But then, I hadn't seen her in anything but blurred and distant pictures: Me and the boys at the State Fair.

"Cat got your tongue?"

"Now, Judy."

"I'll keep the Judith, thank you. Is this the best you could do?" She meant the table.

I come to the Russian Tea Room for lunch not less than twice a week. I get a great table, have for years. I'd just thought little Judy Kronske, she'll be frumpy, maybe a little loud with that terrible Midwestern twang....

The twang had disappeared. I asked for a gin and tonic— I always drink Pellegrino at lunch—and I desperately considered new strategies. Throw myself on her mercy. She didn't look like she had any. She looked like Catherine, the blue-blooded, ice-cold heroine of *Diamond Heart* and a little like Justine, the chilly adventuress from *Emerald Eyes*.

"You're staring."

"What happened to...?"

"The weight? The glasses? The tuh-wang?"

"Yes."

"They were an invention, Margaret."

"*What?*"

"I'd researched you, Margaret."

Judith sipped Pellegrino and nibbled at the crudités. I was feeling queasy. My drink came just as Judith told me.

"I researched you, Margaret. I knew you were a great agent. I wanted desperately for you to take me on. *Quality, not quantity* appealed to me. I thought, Find out what they eat and feed it to them. You're from where? Pittsburgh? It gave me a twang. You had an alcoholic father, a cheating husband—I gave me those. I invented what you left behind, someone you could feel superior to."

"Judith, this isn't funny."

"Sure it is. Lighten up...Peggy."

"Judith," I lied sweetly, "I'm willing to work things through."

AND BABY MAKES THREE

Casting Call

[RODNEY] The Greta Garbo of gay men. Drop-dead gorgeous in his youth and still as glamorous as his famous clients, the only thing better than his taste is his skill....LEAD (84)

AND BABY MAKES THREE

"**S**he had lovely hair." That's what I always say whenever they ask me about Baby. This is true and it's a charming thing to say. I believe in being charming.

Let me introduce myself. I am Rodney Ludonoff, the hairdresser to the stars. I've done them all—Marilyn, Judy, Bette, Rita, Joan. The real stars knew what they wanted—stardom—and knew that I could help give it to them. God knows, I tried.

Not that it showed. "Make it look easy," my great friend Sydney always told me. "And if you can't say something nice, don't say anything at all."

I took Sydney's advice. Faced with a bulging forehead, I designed signature bangs "to show off those eyes." Sabotaged by a lantern chin, I created an updo, to balance the barracuda smile and "show off this swan neck." Doughy from booze, hopped up on amphetamines? I gave them soufflés of lightly lifted curls designed to "catch that little-girl-lost appeal."

I was a master tactician. "Make them feel pretty," Sydney always advised me. I gave them pink silk smocks, surrounded them with fresh peonies, roses and lilacs. My working bungalow was always a haven of peace, serenity and femininity. We had fun. "You always smell so good," I would say. "It's such a treat to work on you."

They believed me. Hung over, rank with sweat from the stage lights, they believed me. Were they hiding behind the door when God handed out IQs and noses? I nearly believed me myself.

"You're a genius, Rodney," they would say. As well they should have. A well-placed curl disguised a marital bruise.

An asymmetrical bang drew attention from the pop-eyed stare, exactly like a Boston terrier's. The scoop of a pageboy softened a jaw.

The first time I met Baby, she was still a little girl—and not a pretty one. Her mother, a great beauty and truly a lady, was one of my favorites. Her intractable, *beloved* child was a constant wound. It isn't easy for celebrity children, but it isn't exactly impossible either. Just nearly. Look at Liza Minnelli, Jane Fonda—Michael Douglas, for that matter. Baby *was* impossible.

"She terrifies me, Rodney," her mother confided. "Where will she stop? I don't know what to do with her. I gave her a kitten and she killed it. She dresses her puppies like dolls until the poor things whimper and go limp from the heat. She's such a little bully."

"Get her a pony," I suggested. "A pony's bigger than she is."

The pony quickly went lame.

At twelve, Baby affected her mother's wardrobe and began a competition that went beyond mere adolescence. At sixteen, she stole her mother's lover, a very famous man. At seventeen, she aborted his baby and nearly shipwrecked her mother's career.

"Every time I get a job, she has an emergency. I've been called from the set the very first day—*twice*."

"Timing's everything," I suggested.

"You don't think? Rodney! No. She loves me. My Baby loves me." The mere thought of what I implied made her eyes twin pools of terror and pain. "She must love me, mustn't she? I love her."

"I'm sure she does, insomuch as she is capable of loving anybody."

Her mother forgave it all. Motherhood is a marvelous thing. So is denial.

"Can you work with my hair?" Baby pleaded with me whenever I came to the house to work on her mother.

"You have lovely hair," I told her firmly.

"Make it blond. Do something," she begged. What I wanted to do was spank her.

"Could she be trying to drive me crazy?" her mother wondered.

"I don't know," I told her honestly.

The year Baby turned twenty-one, her mother won an Oscar. It brought her a flood of much-deserved attention. Baby took it badly. She decided to act. All she needed was the right vehicle, one that would capitalize on her talents. She was sure that she had them and so was her mother. In fact, her mother had tried to share center stage with her since Baby was old enough to warble a note, much less act. From my perspective, it might be a relief to have her dramas on screen. All Baby needed was the right role to break through.

The first I heard of Baby's breakthrough role was a midnight phone call from a producer, a friend of mine, you could say, and a notorious womanizer.

"Rodney. How are you?"

"Sleepy!"

"Rodney. The night is young."

"Only if you're still trying to score, Barry. What can I do for you?"

"A favor. A big favor."

"Barry, this conversation is a favor. It's midnight."

"When did you get so stuffy, Rodney?"

"Ever since I gave up Les Boys."

I gave up Les Boys at forty. I still looked thirty, mind you, but I had a horror of becoming one of those dirty old men, always passing their companions off as nephews. When I gave up Les Boys, I lost touch with Barry. A sex addict—a connoisseur, he'd say—with an avid taste for the younger set, Barry preferred girls to boys but was willing to compromise for a good party. If Barry was calling me at midnight, something was up. I would guess his cock.

"You haven't said yes. I want you to do my next picture."

"That's employment, Barry, not an emergency. What aren't

you telling me?"

"I'll pay you double."

"Barry?"

"Oh, all right. My girlfriend's the lead. She won't take no for an answer about you. It's in her contract."

Clearly, Barry had himself over a barrel. He'd promised something he couldn't deliver. Namely, me. Even at a normal hour, I'd have found it tiresome. At midnight, I found it unbearable.

"No, Barry," I told him.

"I don't think you understand me, Rodney."

"Maybe not. We'll talk tomorrow."

I did understand Barry and that's why I said we'd talk. I understood Barry even without hearing the feminine query, "What did he say?" as we hung up the phone.

Barry. Over the years I've watched him move from cheating on his wife to cheating on his girlfriends to cheating on his friends. If Barry gets a hard-on for something or somebody, there's no stopping him. It was now 12:45, long past bedtime for those of us who work, but I found sleep was now impossible. Barry was a nightmare. I called Rosannah, my agent and closest friend of twenty years.

"Rosannah? It's Rodney. I'm sorry to call so late—really—but Barry, *that* Barry, just called me and is determined I do his next movie."

"And you declined?"

"No. I said I'd get back to him."

"Oh, good. I thought this was an emergency. We'll handle it tomorrow."

"You're sure?"

"Even Barry can wait one night, Rodney."

"You're sure?"

"Sweet dreams."

Despite Rosannah's assurances, I did not have sweet dreams. I dreamed of dismembered cats, dogs, even ponies. In short, I dreamed of Barry. Barry who stopped at nothing to get his way. My friend Claude, a set designer, once declined Barry's request that he do a period movie for him. The period was the 1920s, the place, Seattle, the schedule inconvenient. Claude declined and a week later received his fox terrier in the mail. She had been missing since the day he said no to Barry.

Claude's wasn't the only story. A lovely actress of a certain age, determined to deter Barry's advances on her daughter, received a muff made from her Himalayan cat. The note read *Why fight over a little pussy?*

I had no pets, unless you counted my prize roses, and I should have slept soundly, but I had the uncomfortable feeling that Barry was only part of the story. I'd only heard the woman's voice over the phone, darkly, but I could have sworn I knew the woman whispering in Barry's ear. But who?

My phone rang at seven. It was Rosannah. Sounding uncharacteristically rattled.

"Rise and shine."

"Rosannah?"

"He's schtupping Baby."

So, that was it. The voice I'd heard was Baby's. No wonder my nightmares were raining cats and dogs. No wonder my agent sounded shaken. Barry *and* Baby? I'd be lucky to survive.

Rosannah dipped into her counselor's voice, a specialty among good agents. "I think we should fight a war of containment with Baby," she advised me.

"That's like trying to enforce a limited nuclear arms agreement."

"You're right. Oh, Rodney, what is it with her?"

I offered my theory. I'd had years to think about it, years of counseling her mother on bringing up Baby. As I saw it, Baby was a creature of her own device. The Bad Seed with a good cover story—her mother.

"She's a victim," I told Rosannah, "or, at least, she thinks she is."

Rosannah sighed. "You're right. We all know what a terrible childhood she thinks she had...."

It was true. We all knew about Baby's much-vaunted pain. It was her excuse for everything.

"Victims are always the most dangerous," I said, expanding my theory.

"Why is that?"

"They're victims. They believe they are justified in doing anything—it's all self-defense."

"Well...the bottom line is...she wants you."

"I'm gay, Rosannah."

"This is serious." We both knew it was.

"So am I. I don't want anywhere near that woman."

"Who does? Why are we acting like we have a choice? Let me tell you the story." Rosannah took a long asthmatic breath. Her asthma was stress related, and this was stress.

"Calm down, Rosannah." This had the sound of a major attack.

"I am calm. I'm just succumbing to blackmail."

"You?"

"I got a set of pictures this morning," she told me. "I'm calling you from the car. I need to stop by."

Rosannah arrived armed with a box of doughnuts. She nibbled while we talked in the little rose garden just outside my study. I worked on my roses while Rosannah gave me the gory details.

"Remember when Rafael and I were separated?" She nervously twirled a strand of her signature Titian (my doing) mane.

Rafael was her husband, the love of her life. Yes, I remembered their separation. Rosannah had delivered an ultimatum about his drinking. Raffy had responded by moving out. Rosannah went more than a little crazy—drinking too much herself, even managing a brief, catastrophic affair.

"They have pictures."

"What?"

"Of me and that—that boy. I should have known when Barry introduced us he was up to something."

"You mean Danny Figaro?"

"Yes."

"That boy was a gigolo."

"Exactly. I had no idea."

Danny Figaro, the gigolo, was young, gifted and black—although he persisted in claiming Italian descent. He was also much more talented than his behaviors would suggest. He was sleeping his way up a ladder he could have climbed by talent alone. The poor kid didn't know that and Barry wasn't about to tell him. Instead, he groomed him into a sort of sexual alter ego, using him, as with Rosannah, to even up scores or gain leverage. Rosannah had a nose for talent, and that, more than a sweet tooth, drew her to Danny.

As an agent, Rosannah was a natural shark. As a woman, she was a little plump, still pretty, but at the other end of the food chain—at least in Los Angeles. She was a woman a Latin would appreciate, and a Latin was what she had found. Her marriage to Rafael, a Brazilian, afforded her a fortress to flirt and tease from, but she was really far more naive than her speech or reputation suggested. She was a womanly woman in a man's game.

"I talk a good game," she once admitted to me, scandalized because a married actor on the rise had made a very serious pass. In her grief, she was a sitting duck for Danny and Barry.

During their separation, I had seen Rafael. He was two weeks sober, a newcomer to A.A., eager to reconcile with his wife but still struggling to maintain a precarious sobriety. He'd asked me to lunch.

"How is she?"

"How are *you*?"

"Fine. Better. I miss her. Have you seen her? Is she dating anyone?"

"Raffy, I'm not at liberty."

"Do you think she'll take me back?"

I thought she would and I told Rafael as much. We were lunching at Ma Maison on very credible salade Niçoise and, aside from a few wayward glances at passing bottles of wine, lunch was a pleasant affair. New as his sobriety was, I thought it would stick.

Sworn to secrecy for thirty days, I nonetheless importuned Rosannah to drop her ill-considered lover and spend a few weeks taking care of herself, just feathering the nest and plumping pillows. "You don't think he's coming back?" she pressed me. "Is he sober? Oh, Rodney, you don't know what that would mean to me...."

But I did know and was delighted when Rosannah dropped her gigolo and the ten extra pounds she'd gained dealing with her nibbling fears. Rafael's sobriety and their subsequent reconciliation were now established facts, but with these pictures...

The pictures had come by special messenger. Fortunately for Rosannah, they arrived while Rafael was at his early-bird A.A. meeting. There was a large gray envelope, twenty-four pictures of Danny and Rosannah—eight-by-ten glossies—and a note: *Rodney's being stubborn.*

Rosannah was not just my agent. She was my closest friend of twenty years. We were like brother and sister. We would have done anything for each other—which was precisely the point.

"That was it? No blackmail demand?" I was dismayed to see some tiny aphids at work on my Tiffany rose. I would need to remedy that. Could Barry be importing aphids into my rose garden?

"Rodney? The pictures are blackmail."

Of course they were! Obviously, the pictures came from Barry.

They could endanger Rosannah's precarious happiness and would be withheld from use only if I cooperated with him.

"What did you do?" As if I didn't know.

"Obviously, I called Barry and committed you. You do her hair; they're out of mine. That's the deal."

"And what if I say no?" Not that I ever would, and we all knew that.

"Simple." Rosannah picked a dead rose from its moorings. "You would break my heart, ruin my marriage, endanger Rafael's newly found sobriety..."

"Rosannah, that's blackmail."

"It's also the truth. Rodney, I will owe you."

"Nonsense. Hand me that funny little scissors and I'll make you a bouquet for your dressing table. And get the negatives."

Baby's first day on set, her call was at six A.M. for an eight o'clock start. She got there by neither. Now, her mother had been notoriously late, so a certain amount could be laid to conditioning. But Baby's mother had a charm and grief about her tardiness. I saw it as fear—a debilitating fear of failure—and so I found it inconvenient and yet somehow forgivable.

In Baby, the same tardiness felt different. In Baby, late felt like arrogance. Late felt like "Fuck you all. I am the star."

She entered my bungalow, demanding a Coca-Cola. "Bad for the camera," I warned her. "Sugar bloat." I offered black coffee, very strong, and a plain baguette with apricot jam from my own tree. Baby turned up her nose.

"You're late," I told her, working in her shampoo. Her hair was dull from cigarette smoke and dry from her alcohol consumption. "And you need to be drinking a lot of water."

"I overslept."

"Time is money, Baby."

"So work fast, Uncle Rodney."

I did work fast. And it took every ounce of my professionalism not to work roughly.

"Ouch!" This from Baby when Barry stuck his head through the door. "You hurt me! Barry, he's taking forever. I'm sorry."

"Just remember you asked for him," Barry told her. Baby gave him the finger.

Say what you will, they were a match made in heaven. I've long had a theory that evil, like severe illness, has a distinctive wavelength. You can feel it. I hated touching Baby. I felt a repugnance at soul level. The schedule was twelve weeks long and I personally planned to take a prolonged vacation in Maui as soon as we wrapped. Let the Great Kahuna purge my evil spirits. At least, look at some waves that were not permanent.

Barry and Baby were doing a remake of *South Pacific*—sex roles switched. Baby played a WAVE, which allowed her to capitalize on her mother's screen image from the forties. It was a shrewd career move—and theft, if you asked me. Was nothing sacred? Did Baby really think she could build her career banking on her mother's talents and goodwill? (Yes. And she was right.) I resented her nerviness.

"You don't like me," Baby lamented late one evening. We'd been shooting for fourteen hours, and fatigue made me candid.

"No," I said. "I don't. I don't like your behavior."

"You mean late? My mother was late."

"Your mother was your mother. Sit still!"

"I've heard that my whole life. I want you to do my hair like Mama's for the Bali sequence. Can you do that? Make me look like my mother?"

I could do that, but it would take some artistry. Although blessed with her mother's luminous eyes, Baby more closely resembled her father, not a handsome man.

"Can you?"

"Yes, I can."

"I told Barry you could!" Baby was triumphant.

I wondered what else Baby told Barry. Her dalliance with Janos, our director of photography, was becoming ever more evident. Now, all leading ladies—certainly the smart ones—make a point of cultivating their director of photography. In the old days, many teamed up going film to film, collaborating on the screen image that became their mutual obsession. Inevitably, there was a certain frisson of sexual energy to such collaborations: Beauty and the Beast; Beauty opening herself to the dark Cyclopean eye of the lens. Baby took this flirtation a step further—stupidly, I felt. Wasn't the element of imagination best maintained for the screen?

Barry, besotted in a way I'd never seen him, allowed Baby her fling. I found this acceptance vulgar, but then, Barry and Baby were vulgar.

"It's just good business," I actually heard Baby tell Barry as she stepped out of her trailer after a long lunch-hour "lighting conference" with Janos.

I must have rolled my eyes. To me she said, "Those wild Hungarians. Such romantics—and they do love their drink." Who was she kidding?

"So do you," I told her. I took her by the elbow and led her into my bungalow. She didn't like it a bit. The minute we were in the door she turned on me.

"For God's sake, Uncle Rodney. Mama drank. Why is it everything she did was fine and everything I do isn't?"

"Your mother was a lady."

"A lady? My mother fucked *her* cameraman."

"Never. He admired her. They were friends with a yearning, nothing more."

"Is that what she told you? What a joke. Besides, sex is just a technicality. Just a technicality."

Baby was drunk and repeating herself. Did she think I didn't know about the bottle of Grand Marnier in her outsize purse? Did she think I missed her coke habit even though she carried a rock the size of the Ritz in a little velvet pouch? Who was she kidding? Her drinking showed. Her drugging showed—if not on her, on Janos. He'd gone from a good-looking man to a haggard one, and it wasn't just the rigors of the period shoot. It was Baby. Just like Barry, Janos was hooked on her. Just like Barry, Janos was paying a price. What does she do? I wondered. She was leggy, flat-hipped, even boyish. Did she fulfill some homosexual fantasy? As an avowed homosexual myself, I prefer womanly women, feminine ones like Baby's mother. Or Rosannah.

"She's into kink," one rumor about Baby had it.

"She's into bondage," ran another.

What is the difference between kink and bondage? I wondered.

"Guns," Rosannah told me.

The production ran its catastrophic course. The cameraman on drugs. The producer looking equally strung out. Baby, gloating, in the center of it all—a real crazy maker. Couldn't she see she was hurting the movie? Probably not. Janos made her look like an angel. Barry and the director gave her thirty takes if she needed them. The editor was a genius. No doubt, the movie would make Baby a star to be reckoned with. It could have happened to a much nicer girl.

"This is important. Meet me at Le Dôme."

I knew a summons when I heard one. Particularly when it came from Rosannah and woke me from a dead sleep on Sunday, our one day off in a six-day schedule. And so, I met Rosannah at noon, still blinking sleep from my eyes.

"Thanks for coming out," Rosannah looked flushed—with

excitement or panic, I could not tell which. The maître d' settled us at an airy four top with a view of the Strip—Rosannah's clout, not mine. Rosannah drummed the powder-puff tablecloth with her scarlet nails, waiting until we were alone.

"This is serious. More pictures have surfaced," she whispered breathlessly.

This was serious. I was already working for Barry. If they were talking money...

"You didn't get the negatives?" Rosannah shook her head from side to side. "They're asking money?" She grew more vehement. "What? You had another affair?"

"No, no, no!" To my relief, Rosannah was laughing. Somehow, I had misunderstood.

"*I* have the pictures," she said. "Pictures of Baby and Danny Figaro. Current pictures."

"She's sleeping with him too? Baby makes three!"

Rosannah gave me a look reserved for visiting aunts from Dubuque. "C'mon, Rodney. You've heard the stories—twosomes, threesomes, then-somes. She sleeps with everybody, Rodney. The point is, she promised Danny a part in Barry's movie, then didn't deliver."

The light slowly dawned. "So he took the pictures to Barry?"

It was the wrong light, evidently. "No way!" Rosannah snorted. "Barry's in love with Baby. He'd have killed Danny. Danny brought the pictures to me."

"But he's already blackmailing you."

Rosannah gave me the Dubuque look again. "Rodney, Barry was blackmailing me. Danny and I were victims."

"Believe that, you believe anything," I warned her.

A bottle of Taittinger arrived and a silver pitcher of orange juice. We were clearly celebrating, but just what? Wasn't it a little premature? Our waiter hovered as unobtrusively as a helicopter over Bel-Air. We took the hint and ordered—pesto omelettes, fresh strawberries, arugula salads with mandarin oranges and walnuts. When the busboy belatedly graced us with water—the most expensive commodity in L.A.—Rosannah got to the point.

"Danny thought I might have use for the pictures."

"I see."

"And I might." Rosannah buttered a fresh brioche and slathered it with blackberry jam. I waited until she enjoyed two large bites, then nudged her.

"Don't tell me you're holding a grudge against poor old Barry?" I asked.

"Don't tell me you're not holding a grudge against Baby?" Rosannah hefted her mimosa. "To revenge," she toasted.

I hate inflicting pain and, to tell you the truth, I did feel guilty. Not for hurting Baby—may her creme rinse never work on tangles—but for hurting Janos. Poor Janos. He arrived at set the next morning looking ashen and subdued. Rosannah had delivered the photos by special messenger the night before. Baby was right about one thing. Hungarians *are* romantic, and Janos was clearly brokenhearted by her betrayal.

What is it with cinematographers? They see everything and nothing. Focused on their composition, they can be blind to content. Perched on cranes at dizzying heights, they are utterly impervious to danger. Janos, devoted to making Baby an icon of screen loveliness, had mistaken his craft for her character, his image of her for real life. Just like the public.

Baby. Everybody in town knew she was trouble. Everyone had a story about her. There was the three-day affair with the guy who painted her pool house. The driver who got lucky on the way to the Academy Awards. Hadn't Janos heard the stories? Was he deaf as well as blind?

"Good morning, Janos," I offered as we bumped elbows at the craft service table.

"Good morning, Rodney. Is she here yet?"

"Baby? How could she be here? That would be on time," I joshed him.

"Yes, true. My mistake." Janos laughed weakly. I could imagine the photographs he'd received. Kink. Bondage. Did an unpleasant image hurt a visual person more than a normal man? I would guess yes. Janos certainly looked fatally wounded. I hit on a plan.

"Janos? Could I interest you in a moment's conversation?"

Docile as a lamb, Janos followed me numbly to my work bungalow. I offered him a chair. He accepted the chair. His hands were shaking.

"Hung over?" I inquired. "Migraine? Flu? You look terrible."

"Thanks." He accepted three aspirin and a glass of water.

"But you've been making Baby look wonderful—like an angel." Janos sighed. "That's my job."

I sighed too. "And mine...lest I forget." He looked at me sharply.

"You don't like Baby?"

"Well..."

Janos and I shared a rueful laugh. I could see him relaxing, deciding to confide.

"You don't like her?" he repeated.

"Janos, she has lovely hair," I answered. "But..."

She's so sad. She needs to be healed."

"Then she should stop being one."

"One?" Janos didn't get the joke.

"A heel."

"Ah!" He gave me a small smile. "You really don't like her." Now it was a statement, flat, as he tested what felt like thin ice.

"No. If people can't have morals, they should at least have manners."

Janos conceded the point.

We talked for hours. Baby was very late that morning. When she arrived for work, I offered her a Coke Classic, hoping for sugar bloat. Adjusting a bang on an unflattering angle, I assured her, "You have lovely hair."

At dailies the next day, I noticed the slightest shift in Janos' shooting style. Baby's weak chin was somehow emphasized. Her protuberant lower lip—previously a Barcalounger for desire— now looked a touch pendulous, a little bit unpleasant.

"Did you change something?" Barry asked me. We were screening in the little old room at MGM, the one way up by the catwalks. It was a terrible room.

"Not really," I told him. After all, what was half an inch off a bouffant among friends? (About five years in age up on the screen.)

"She looks tired or something," Barry complained.

The "or something" was the tiniest shift of a temple wave, altering it from languorous to tough. That, together with the slightest lowering of Janos' usual angle on her wavery chin, rendered Baby less luscious and more over the hill.

"Maybe you're tired, Barry," I told him. "Are you two up all night like a couple of kids?"

Barry winced. So did Janos. I knew I'd hit a sore spot.

"She wanted to stay in and run her lines last night," he told me. "I was in bed by nine at my place. Alone."

"A first, I'm sure."

"Yeah, yeah." Barry waved off the reference to his prodigal ways. "Well, you two think she looks right?"

"Fine."

"Fine," Janos agreed.

Baby was not allowed in dailies. It wasn't like she was De Niro and could actually use them to calibrate adjustments. Barry didn't want to make her nervous. As a result, Baby did not know how bad things were looking for her with Janos. How bad she was looking herself.

"What do you think?" Janos asked me after Barry left the screening room. "She's..." He searched for words.

"She's not a nice girl," I told him.

"No."

"She's vulgar, petty, dishonest, disloyal, unattractive, and immoral. And she uses people," I added.

"Yes," Janos allowed finally. "She does."

"And a picture is worth a thousand words," I urged him on.

"Yes," he agreed. Our eyes met to seal the deal. We were conspirators.

ROLL OVER

Casting Call

[MASSEUR] Think young Rock Hudson—a hunk with a heart of gold. The kind of straight-arrow gay man who makes straight seem unattractive....LEAD (102)

ROLL OVER

You'd think people would know better. Maybe not. Still, I am always amazed by what they choose to tell me.

"You've got magic fingers" it starts out. You'd think I was a call girl. Maybe in some ways I am.

"It's better than an orgasm," I once had a movie star tell me, and judging from her reputation, she should know. I'll try to be discreet about this, but you may still know her—porcelain skin, sunlit hair, cheekbones like cliffs—not to mention the accents. I've worked on her through three accents. Formal, nearly anonymous. When she told me my work was better than an orgasm, I just said, "Thank you, ma'am."

"Not 'ma'am.' I hate 'ma'am.'"

"What should I call you, then?"

"Mmm. I suppose 'Miss.' Oh, oh, that's heaven. Heaven. Do it again. Deeper. Deeper if you can. Oh."

No, it was not an orgasm. It was the sound she made when I unkinked her left shoulder, the one she'd strained lugging her wounded movie husband back inside their log cabin. What a hunk he was. A country and western singing star who crossed over to movies via the soaps. All he needed was a big break and she planned to give it to him.

"What do you think of him?" she asked me.

"I wouldn't kick him out of bed."

"That's what I meant. He's that sexy, isn't he? It's not just me."

"I think before you it was all of Nashville and the entire readership of *The National Enquirer*."

"Not exactly my peer group, but I'll let that pass."

"Roll over."

"Roll over, please."

"Here I'm the star."

"You're so manly."

The truth is, I am manly and it is a help in my line of work. I know there are fat masseurs and thin masseurs and black, white, red, yellow and mixed masseurs, but I am the current reigning masseur to the stars, and it's a big help that I'm better looking than they are. Even if I say so myself. Six foot three, ice-blue eyes, prematurely white hair the color of new snow, striking, which is sometimes where they want to take things, but I have my standards.

"Oh. Jesus. Again. Just one more time."

If I ran a tape recorder I could make a fortune off my clients' sighs and whispers.

My movie star whispered now. "He is divine, isn't he?"

"I thought you were happy with her, the craft service girl, the animal wrangler from Topanga."

"Who told you that? What an ugly rumor."

"You. You told me."

"Oh. Do I tell you everything?"

Most clients did, sooner or later, and so Miss Movie Star had told me about her happy love affair, the one she was about to jeopardize for the sake of a little publicity.

"Don't do it." Her poor girlfriend!

"I'm not going to actually fuck him. I don't think I am." She giggled, an unpleasant sound not in her films. "We'll pretend to fuck and if he falls in love, he'll get over it. They all do."

"Has he agreed to your little scheme?"

"He will. He wants to be a star."

"Roll over." I gave her a little swat. I always told my clients I ask them to roll over to keep them limber. The truth is, I ask them to roll over when I don't want them to see my shocked little Midwestern face. I may be the masseur to the stars, but I grew up in Omaha, where the closest thing we have to a celebrity is a novelist you may have heard of, Judith Muir. I know about her because one of her twin sons knocked up my first cousin, a fiasco that blessedly ended in a miscarriage, drug-induced. Her family is known for that sort of thing, and that is blamed on her connection to Hollywood—a thrilling mini-series every single year.

"Roll over," I said to my pliant movie star because I couldn't help sympathize with "him," Rock, the hunk she was about to make famous. To be honest, I knew him, at least by sight to nod hello. We both worked out at Hard Bodies Gym, where, for a gay man like me, the hardest thing was lusting after a straight man like him. Once, truth be told, we even talked as we rowed shoulder to shoulder.

"Hard work, isn't it?" he panted.

"Pays off," I'd answered, positive my lust for him was audible in both syllables.

"I'm supposed to get gorgeous," he chatted on.

"Shouldn't be a stretch." There I went again.

"I've got a part opposite—" He named my movie star client. "I hope she's nice."

"What do you care?"

"I'm nervous."

I'd have married him right then, he was so charming, and maybe that's why I pummeled my client with a little extra vigor when she told me her scheme. I slapped her for him.

"Ouch!"

"No pain, no gain."

"Do you think I have cellulite?"

"God has cellulite."

"God's not on screen. Just lie to me, for Chrissake. That's why we pay you."

"You're gorgeous, inside and out," I lied obligingly.

"Then he'll want me?"

"Who doesn't?"

As you might gather, it was time to wash my mouth out with soap, but instead I stuffed it with cotton. If she wanted to talk, let her.

"You know how it works in this business. You're only as hot as people think you are. Now I'm very hot, but I could always be more so, right?"

"Right."

"I mean, business is business and she'll just have to understand, right?"

"So you're going to tell her?"

"That's not my style."

"Roll over."

It was two weeks later, on my way into Hard Bodies, that I ran into him. He looked exhausted—not a great look for a would-be movie star.

"How's it going?" I asked.

"Not great."

"What's the problem?"

"Are you from here?"

"Is anybody?"

"I'm from West Virginia."

"I'm from Omaha."

"Omaha. Are people nicer there?"

"Maybe."

"Want a smoothie?"

It's not my style to ask a straight man for drinks, but he seemed desperate. I wondered if my movie star had anything to do with it.

"I could do that. Yeah."

And so we ordered a Citrus Sunset and Boysenberry Blush

and carried them out to the hot tub.

"Hollywood," he said.

"What about it?"

"I'm having this fake tabloid affair with a movie star, and her girlfriend's the one I'm in love with."

"The plot thickens."

"I'm over my head. I mean, she's a confirmed lesbian. She says kissing me's politically incorrect."

"She's kissing you? Maybe she's a hasbian."

"What's that?"

"That's a lesbian who switched teams."

"Teams?"

"Oh, you really are from West Virginia."

"You mean sexual preferences? Can people switch?"

"Yes, you said she's kissing you."

"I'm kissing her."

"She's kissing back?"

"She says she's in love with this movie star. The one that's supposed to be in love with me."

"But she's kissing you?"

"Yes. She did last night. What should I do?"

Oh, the power. I squinted thoughtfully. I stared west toward the sunset, which, at the moment, was gilding my companion's features so he looked like a Greek god. What a mensch he was. What a bitch my movie star was. What a matchmaker I was. It seemed only fair.

"Kiss her some more," I said. "Call me politically incorrect, but kiss her some more. If I were a lesbian, I'd fall for you."

"Thank you. I better get going. I've got a one o'clock call."

That's what I love about people from West Virginia. They still have manners. When he and his hasbian got married one Sunday afternoon in Topanga, they remembered to invite me.

"Kiss her some more," I shouted, a little carried away with myself when he finally kissed the bride, wreathed in smiles and a rosy boa constrictor.

MY NEW LIFE

Casting Call

[HONEY] A feisty, ardent dreamer who wears blue
jeans and cowboy boots, her heart on her sleeve and a
Panaflex under her arm....LEAD (110)

MY NEW LIFE

$$\frown\frown$$

My new life began about ten miles west of the Pecos River. That is where I said to Jerry, "Pull over—now."

Jerry pulled the car, a black BMW coupe with tinted windows, onto the shoulder. Route 10 had broad, sloping shoulders—just like the Texans we'd just fought about in the Texaco truck stop.

"Will you look at this?" Jerry said as we entered the truck stop, and then, "Stop staring." *He* was the one who was staring.

The truck stop was done up in red, white and blue, with a phone in every booth and a special booth reserved for "professional drivers on a time schedule." There was an ample supply of books on tape, the trucker's legal amphetamine, plus Willie Nelson tape collections and Gulf War T-shirts. Jerry was the only man I saw wearing a Rolex or leather Adidas.

"Unbelievable, huh?" Jerry whispered loudly. He nodded toward a booth where a father and son duo in matching Stetsons and matching faces stared back at us.

"I imagine that's what they're thinking of us," I said.

"Why do you say that?" Jerry asked—as I'd known he would.

"Well, let's see... You're wearing a three-thousand-dollar watch, a ten-dollar black T-shirt, ninety-dollar jeans and three-hundred-dollar shoes—with one earring and a purse."

"Shoulder bag," Jerry corrected me. "Camera bag, really."

"Right. What about the black T-shirt, the watch, the beard?"

"C'mon. They all dress like this." By "they" Jerry meant Lucas, Scorsese, Spielberg—his pantheon of personal heroes. For a while, they had dressed like that and so had every aspiring filmmaker in America. No wonder the directors were shaving their beards, trading their T-shirts for Armanis. Personally, I suspected that none of them had ever been as humorless and self-important as their clones.

"There's a phone in every booth. It's like the Polo Lounge, for Chrissake," Jerry sniggered. To my knowledge, Jerry had never been in the Polo Lounge—yet.

"That's so the truckers can phone ahead or call home."

"Okay," Jerry said, "but who'd want to wait home for him?"

He hooked a thumb toward the young, overweight trucker in a *Star Wars* T-shirt who was punching in a song on the jukebox. "He looks more like a steer than a cowboy." Patsy Cline came on the jukebox.

"Good taste in music," I said, nodding slightly to the young trucker, who winked at me. Try as I had, I could never master the dead cool of my East Village friends. Men flirted with me like they might with the truck-stop waitress in Indiana, where I grew up.

"I hate this shit," Jerry said. "Did he wink at you?"

"Maybe."

I was tired of protecting Jerry's ego. Tired of his paranoia about other men. Tired period—first trimester, my gynecologist said. For two years, I'd steered clear of other men and Jerry's jealousy. Today, I thought, let him get pounded.

Jerry was my boyfriend of two years, three months, the time it had taken me to get my MFA in film. Jerry had his doctorate and a development deal at Universal, which was why we were driving to L.A.

I, not Jerry, had won a Student Academy Award for my documentary on cowboys at Madison Square Garden, but it was agreed between us that it was a fluke and he was the serious filmmaker.

"He looks like something out of your little movie," Jerry said, squinting meaningfully at the tall-drink-of-water cowboy coming in the door. He looks like heaven, I thought. Was it my pregnancy that was making me sentimental for cowboys and my brilliant career?

"How far along are you?" Jerry asked when I told him that I was pregnant.

"Just a little."

"There's no such thing as 'just a little.' You are or you aren't."

"Not long, I meant. First trimester."

"Ah." He sounded relieved.

"Do you want me to get an abortion?"

"Do you want to?" He sounded more than relieved, eager.

"No," I said, not sure.

"Well, uh, all I meant was, I wouldn't stand in your way."

"C'mon, Jerry. What you meant is you don't want the baby."

"It is bad timing. You've got to admit that—with my movie deal and all."

"Yes, I suppose it is."

I had not wanted an argument. I could feel the tumblers in my head clicking into place. Just like a Vegas slot machine, Jerry was coming up lemons.

"You must be so excited," Judy, my best female friend, had said when I told her the news—that we were going to L.A., that Jerry had a deal, that I was going to have a baby.

"About the baby, you mean?"

"That too," Judy said, "but actually, I meant about the deal and the move. What part of L.A., do you know yet?"

"Jerry's thinking Toluca Lake. It's near the studio. I heard there's a place just past Malibu, where they have ranches."

"You and your cowboys."

"You sound just like Jerry."

In fact, Jerry was sounding just like Judy.

"You and your cowboys," he was saying in the Texaco truck stop. "That guy is staring at you."

I looked. The guy was staring at me. Of course he was!

It was Toby.

"Toby!" I flew across the truck stop to his booth. "Toby!"

"Hi, honey." Toby had called me "honey" the entire six months I'd spent filming, at Madison Square Garden and a number of smaller rodeos staged around the East Coast. We had become friends, sharing complaints about missed shots and missed rides. Toby's specialty was roping. Just now, he hugged me, kissed me, held me at arm's length and inspected me. I passed, because he hugged me again.

"Somebody you know?" It was Jerry, of course. Come to interrupt us.

"Of course I know him. It's *Toby*!" I explained.

"*It's Toby*!" Jerry mimicked me.

"This the guy you always told me about?" Toby asked.

"Toby, this is Jerry. Jerry, Toby. You remember. Toby was in my movie."

"I didn't think you were kissing just a generic cowboy." At this, Toby looked straight into Jerry's eyes. Jerry looked away.

"C'mon, you two. Toby, what're you doing here?"

"Honey, I live here. This is Texas. Buck and I are on our way to a little roping contest. What are you doing here?"

"Buck's here? Where?" I was dancing on my feet. "Buck's Toby's horse," I explained to Jerry. "The buckskin."

"What we're doing here," Jerry cut in, "is driving to L.A. Moving to L.A., actually. I've got a deal at Universal to make a picture."

"No kidding. That's just great. What's the picture, honey?"

"No, no," I explained. "It's Jerry's picture. A surfer-vampire picture."

"Actually, it's a metaphor for drugs," Jerry said. I knew that was what he planned to tell *Premiere* magazine in the cover story on him. He'd rehearsed the line on me.

"A vampire picture," Toby said.

"Like Coppola, you know?" Francis Ford Coppola had just

filmed *Bram Stoker's Dracula*. To my knowledge, he had not yet called it a metaphor for drugs.

"Is Buck in his trailer?"

"Unless he's in the little boy's room—right out back. Join me, Jerry?"

"Excuse me, you guys—I've got to go see Buck."

Of all the horses in my film, of all the horses in my life, Buck was my favorite. A big, tawny athlete with a Roman nose and wayward mane, he had a scar over one eye and reminded me of a tough-guy boxer. He had four white stockings—they looked like bandages—and a muzzle of pure velvet. When I found his trailer—sky-blue, rusted and battered—I stood on the bumper and called in to him.

"Hey, Buck. Hey, guy. Remember me?" He turned his head toward me and I whispered softly, "Hi, big guy."

Reaching over the tailgate, I could just pat his rump, scratching him on his sweet spot just above the tail.

"I miss you," I informed him, running a hand over his heart-with-a-broken-arrow brand, somebody's romantic gesture.

"Sometimes I think you're in love with those cowboys," Jerry would say when I was shooting.

"It's movies I'm in love with," I told him and myself. "Movies and you."

"Movies *are* you, you're supposed to say. Haven't I got you trained yet?" (It was a joke.)

"I'm going to L.A., Buck," I told the gentle stallion, stroking his puckered hide.

The buckskin pony I'd had for my 4-H project in Indiana had been smaller and lighter but was also named Buck—most buckskins were. I had loved that pony and now I loved this horse. He had a sweeter temperament than Jerry. That was for sure.

"I am going to L.A. to make a metaphor about drugs," I told the horse's rump. "Actually, to support Jerry while *he* makes a metaphor about drugs. I'm making a baby."

The horse did not reply. Unless you could call the switch of his tail an answer.

"Hey, honey. What you doing talking to a horse's ass?" It was Toby's drawl, the same drawl I'd listened to over and over on the Steenbeck as I edited. This time, he was calling to me from the truck-stop door, not the editing table. "Your boyfriend wants to know if you're going to eat."

"Tell him I'm pregnant."

"What?"

"Tell him I've got morning sickness."

"Hey, that's great!"

Toby was across the parking lot in three long strides. He wrapped his sinewy arms around me right as I stood on the bumper. He smelled of aftershave and liniment. He must have pulled something lately. When his arms went around me, I started to cry.

"Are you eating or what?" Jerry called from the restaurant door. "We can't stay here forever."

"She's sickly," Toby called back. "She's getting some air."

"I've got to go," I said. Toby's shirt smelled like heaven, my heaven anyway—faintly of sweat, faintly of horse, faintly of leather.

"Aw, honey," Toby said. "Maybe you could keep down some country biscuits and gravy. It's like baby food. All white and gooey."

"Maybe."

At the Student Academy Awards, I had thanked Jerry and "all the cowboys in my life," but, by then, the postcards from Alex and Rusty and Ned had stopped coming regularly. Only Toby still called every now and then. If I were honest, there weren't any cowboys in my life any longer, and I missed them—I missed the me I'd been with them, a grown-up version of my Indiana 4-H tomboy.

"Find another subject," Jerry advised me. "Maybe you could make a documentary about me making my movie."

"Maybe I could make fudge brownies too."

"You don't have to be such a bitch. I meant you needed to be shooting. You can find another bunch of freaks to be immersed in."

This was our worst fight, Jerry saying that any man dumb enough to willingly break his bones was a freak and an idiot, I saying I felt the same way around any man who would willingly be caught dead in a Rolex and a Gap T-shirt.

"It's just a style," Jerry defended himself.

"That's the problem," I spat back. "Boots, at least, have a reason."

"Yeah, to make you taller." Jerry was short, but then, so were a number of my heroes.

"To protect against snakebite, to keep your foot from slipping through the stirrup. That's the reason for the heel."

"I know, I know. About how a quarter horse is the fastest horse in the world for a quarter of a mile."

This was supposed to make me laugh and signal it was time to get in bed and make up, but "bed" wasn't as simple as it once was. When did I get pregnant? I wondered. Funny, the pregnancy didn't bother me but Jerry did—was that just hormones?

"What if I named him Nasty?" Jerry asked. I drew a blank. Could he be talking about the baby?

"Who?" I asked.

"My hero. The guy in my movie." Jerry always called it his "movie," not his "script."

"Oh, my Nasty?" I couldn't wait to hear this one.

"For Nosferatu, of course."

"Of course."

Had Jerry always been such a self-centered jerk? Probably. I might not have noticed if I hadn't met my cowboys. What a courtship that had been. The slow wooing of subject and author, the gradual disclosures, the growing trust, and despite the broken bones, the falls, the "spills and chills"—as Toby called them— there had been the courtesy. "Little lady" was hardly my self-image, but it had been nice to feel noticed in a protective way.

"Neanderthals!" my friend Judy had exclaimed. "What do you need to feel protected for? Take a self-defense course."

I had tried to explain that it wasn't my body that felt protected. It was my spirit.

"There's a great course Thursday nights at the fire station," Judy pressed. "We could take it together."

"Maybe I'm just tired of self-centered jerks," I told Judy.

"Cowboys? They're self-centered jerks too," Nellie, a cowgirl, had told me. I was filming her as she zipped into her turquoise chaps, the ones that matched her pinky ring and her eyeliner. "But at least they like horses," she added.

"I like Buck," I volunteered.

"You like Toby—and why not? He's got a soft spot for you."

So, here I was at a Texaco truck stop just west of the Pecos River, sitting in an orange Naugahyde booth with Toby and Jerry.

"When's the blessed event?" Toby asked.

"What?" Jerry asked.

"When's the project due?"

"Oh, I have to deliver the first draft in three months," Jerry said.

"*Her* project," Toby said—with an edge this time.

"Pancakes?" The waitress looked like a weightlifter, huge plates balanced along both arms. Jerry seemed to have ordered in my absence.

"Right here," Jerry said. "Jesus! They're huge."

"That's how we grow 'em, honey," said Cherry, the waitress. She had black curly hair and carefully penciled brows. She looked exactly like her sister Darlene, who was working the register.

"The lady will have biscuits and gravy," Toby said.

"That stuff's like glue," said Jerry. "How can you eat it?"

"I'll have biscuits and gravy too."

We settled into silence until Toby dug out a quarter and played some Patsy Cline. She was "Walking After Midnight."

"Patsy Whine, I call her," Jerry said. Toby gave him a look as level as the Panhandle.

"So, how are you doing this season?" I interjected tactfully—ah, the good little woman.

Jerry looked relieved. Toby talked of takedowns, trophy points, the new five-pound buckle he was wearing.

Jerry leaned over to peek toward Toby's belt. The elaborate buckle featured a roping horse, rider and steer, plus the lettering, raised as a blister, declaring, *Champion.*

"Far out," I said.

"Impressive, huh?" Toby grinned.

"So's a deal at Universal," Jerry muttered.

"What's the liniment for?"

"Buck lost his footing. I was lucky not to undo the knee."

"Right. Toby has had his knee rebuilt twice, but it still pains him," I explained.

"Some," Toby minimized.

"Good pancakes," Jerry said. "Too bad they don't make blintzes."

"This *is* Texas," I said. "West Texas."

"Why, hell, sweetheart. We know what a blintz is here," Toby drawled.

"Funny," Jerry said. "I just have a craving." For the first time he seemed to notice he might be on thin ice.

"She's the one who's supposed to have cravings," Toby chuckled.

"You told him?"

"I was about to upchuck." I felt defensive. "These biscuits and gravy are delicious."

Toby changed the subject.

"Buck threw himself six of the prettiest foals you can imagine —every single one a buckskin or palomino."

"Wait a minute. He's a stallion?" Jerry was bug-eyed. "You crawled halfway in the trailer with a stallion?"

"Gentle as a lamb," Toby said. "Unless he gets an invitation. Then he's a tiger."

I'll bet you are, I thought, then blushed. What's wrong with me? Jerry was glaring.

"You two tying the knot soon, I suppose," Toby supposed.

"We're not sure," I murmured.

"Didn't want to make any major moves until after my movie."

"Seems like a kid is a pretty major move," Toby said.

"If you'd excuse me."

I walked out of the dining room, through the lobby with its map of Texas and rack of tourist brochures and turned into the women's rest room, a big tiled glory with tin sheets tacked to the walls instead of mirrors. In the tin, I looked faint, blurry and out of focus—just like I felt. What am I doing? I asked myself. Then I knew...

I dumped my purse on a small counter marked BABY CHANGING FACILITY and started counting. I ended at three thousand four hundred and forty-three. I separated the four hundred forty-three dollars and slipped it into my jeans. The three thousand, my nest egg, went back into my purse.

I headed back through the dining room to the table, where the two men looked like they needed a translator—or maybe a hired labor consultant.

"Don't leave," I said to Toby, who was on his feet, leaving, by the time I got back.

"*We're* leaving," Jerry said. "Pedal-to-the-metal time."

"I'll see you," I said to Toby, who scooped me up for a final hug. "Watch for me," I whispered in his ear. "Watch real close."

"Sure thing."

"What was that about?" Jerry wanted to know as I dug the four hundred forty-three dollars out of my pocket and he took the entrance merge ramp at seventy-five miles an hour.

"Saying good-bye," I answered.

"Some good-bye," Jerry said.

Buck should just be getting his treat. Toby gave him a sugar packet every time they stopped, I remembered from my film.

"Some good-bye," Jerry repeated, spoiling for a fight.

"Try this one," I said. "Pull over—now."

Stunned, Jerry obeyed me. The BMW went hurtling along the shoulder until it came to a stop. Jerry said something about the first trimester.

"Thanks for the ride," I said. "Good luck. Here's the rest of the trip money." I threw the cash on the seat and opened the door.

"What am I going to do?"

"You'll manage."

I grabbed my duffel bag from the backseat and pulled it through the sunroof. I started waving to Toby as his Dodge Ram truck bore down on me, but then I saw it was already moving onto the shoulder, hauling carefully with the trailer. I ran toward it. Toby opened the door and I scrambled up, lugging my bag. Jerry was sitting in his BMW, staring at us in the rearview mirror.

"What do you want, honey?" Toby asked, his hand on the shift.

"How about some Patsy Whine?" I answered, slamming the door.

Toby pressed a button and then shifted into first.

THE HOUSE OF LOVE

Casting Call

[LADY] If only Bette Davis could tell this story. It's that stubborn, fireball spark of someone who gambled, lost and won anyway. Big eyes, big heart, big dreams....LEAD (122) POSSIBLE NUDITY.

THE HOUSE OF LOVE

⌒⌒

I don't really miss it—my life. Karen, my night nurse, is convinced I should. Meaning, I suppose, that she would—and I'm sure she would, even after all these years.

"Lady, lady, lady, this is no Paris peignoir, this is no fancy-pants Parisienne silk, is it?" she says, tugging my simple cotton shift, light and airy, over my wasted arms.

Parisienne silk is very overrated. You can't live in it, although I once did. My cotton gowns with their sensible tiebacks make me feel like an angel. I'll be one soon enough.

"Lady, lady, lady, this is no cocktail," Karen says, pouring gruel down my throat. My nightcap now is some ghastly concoction of wheat grass and brewer's yeast. It actually tastes a great deal like Fernet Branca, the Sicilian bitters, but without the same punch. Although, why should I worry about punches these days! God knows, I have had enough, quite literally, to last me a lifetime.

Nancy, my day nurse, is more sensible. Nancy is a joy. She heave-hos me into my chair with a tug here or there—she's a little bitty thing—and then off we scoot. Along the lane. Down the road. Push, toodle, push—all the way to the seawall.

How I love this walk. I've loved it since I was a girl and this estate was my father's escape from Hollywood. Nancy loves this walk too. She's a sweet girl, too romantic and pretty to stay with me long. Some young man will fill her head with rubbish and off she'll go. Who could blame her? I went and someday so will she. In the meanwhile, we have these walks. Rides, I should say, at least for me.

"Lady! Lady, look!" Nancy points out a vivid fallen hibiscus beheaded by the night wind.

"Lady, look!" Nancy points now to a lone sea gull cresting the wind. "She looks happy!" Nancy claims. (I have never thought seagulls feminine nor happy, but I don't contradict her. I can't.)

Our walk is a leisurely affair, a stroll really. Nancy is a dawdler, an appreciator, one of God's innocents. "Oh, look!" she cries again and again. It's a caterpillar, a hummingbird, a shy gray lizard. Nancy is a relief to me with her focus on the here and now. We are agreed, she and I, that the present is what we have. The future may yawn ahead of us, uncertain and full of treachery to me, blue and cloudless for my young companion, but here we are. In her innocence, her enthusiasm, her joy in connection, Nancy is my younger self, the self I will stubbornly think of as me, the me before my "accident," as we politely say. Though few people know the truth.

My accident was a long time coming and it began with some very deliberate acts—mine. For one thing, I married him. Yes, I was in love. So what? Swim with the sharks and you get eaten. Tony was a shark.

We met—does this surprise you?—on a yacht. Not my father's. Not mine. His. *That* does surprise you, but you are forgetting that social climbers always dress as the class they aspire to. And Tony was a climber. I know that. I don't blame him for it either. When you're born at the bottom, you either climb or get stepped on. That's what he told me—laughing. He had the whitest teeth. I always thought he should have been an actor.

"I am!" he hooted when I told him, laughing still. We laughed a great deal, Tony and I. Laughed and made love. I'm not sure which I married him for; they were both a novelty for me. As you have guessed, I was born to privilege—which is not a privilege, if you ask me. Tony was born in Hell's Kitchen, "the launching pad," as he called it. His trajectory outward and upward— "away"—carried him straight to me.

I was technically not a virgin, but my sexual experiences had left me emotionally intact, which is to say, quite numb. The boys I knew were quite proper. The one who deflowered me did so at my request. At the time I met Tony, I was still wondering what the big deal was all about. Until I met Tony, I preferred books. A good one was less predictable than a man.

My cousin Joannie introduced me to Tony. Like me, she was a member of the Silver Spoon Set. Unlike me, she'd managed to dent hers up early. Since we were kids, I'd heard stories about how wild she was. When I finally got to know her, at Marymount, I was delighted to find the stories were all true. She did run around with older men. She had sniffed heroin. Her hair was a bottle blond. She had been to Mexico, twice, for abortions. I was fascinated. Joannie enjoyed having a fan. An audience was all she was ever really after.

The day I met Tony, Joannie and I drove to Newport Beach in her roadster. They weren't called convertibles back then. I remember the drive as a giddy rush of images. Joannie drove as fast as she lived. Then too, we were drinking gin fizzes.

"He's my boyfriend, my sometimes boyfriend," she told me about Tony. "He's fun. I couldn't marry him, of course. We'd kill each other. I'll probably marry Stan."

Stan was Joannie's "real" boyfriend, the one with money, education, a background. Stan was dull as a stick, even when he deflowered me. When he settled on Joannie, I was relieved. I'd introduced them on purpose.

"Where'd you meet him?" I asked Joannie, meaning Tony-the-yachtsman.

"Who knows? Maybe a polo game. Yes, a polo game."

"Where'd he go to school?"

"I don't know that he did."

"*Really?*"

At Newport, we found Tony stripped to the waist, toiling over the teak on the yacht he was restoring.

"Like it?" he asked me.

"Like *her*," I corrected him. "Yachts are female."

He said, "No wonder I like rubbing her."

I blushed.

Joannie glanced from one of us to the other.

"I see," she said. "Lets me off the hook. Tony, this is your next heiress, my cousin Lady."

"Lady? Nah!"

"Estelle," Joannie bellowed. I shot her daggers. "No wonder we call her Lady."

"Welcome aboard...Ladies." Tony offered me a hand.

Joannie wasn't interested in second fiddle.

"Have fun, you two. I'm supposed to be meeting Stan anyway. See that she gets home and don't run afoul of my uncle."

"But—" I protested.

"Let her go. She'll get over it," Tony said.

It was as simple as that. Joannie did get over it. Two months later, I was her maid of honor when she married Stan. Tony was not invited, but he didn't seem to care. He went to Catalina for the weekend while I pined and lugged white roses and snowy stephanotis up the aisle, holding my tongue when the minister asked if anyone knew a reason Stan and Joannie should not be united in Holy Matrimony.

Was dull as a stick a reason? Joannie didn't think so. "We balance each other," she said when I asked her at our third bridal fitting. "Tony and I would have killed each other."

"So, I should expect the worst?"

"No. You'll do better. You balance Tony, and besides, he's nobody serious. Just remember that and have fun."

The idea that Tony was no one serious lasted exactly until he kissed me that first afternoon. His kiss closely resembled a body search by the Pasadena police. I told him that.

"You're funny," he said—and kissed me again.

I'd never been kissed like that.

"What is this? A mugging?" I managed.

"Yeah. I like your mug."

That's when our laughs began. As any proper young girl should know, laughter is even more dangerous than sex.

As Mr. Faulkner, one of my father's writers, remarked, we don't really have seasons in Southern California. He was very funny: *A leaf drops in a canyon somewhere and that was fall*, he wrote. Let me tell you about my fall, more colorful than Mr. Faulkner's. If Tony didn't show me the world, he at least showed me its possibilities.

It took me a while to discover that Tony had no "real" home, just a post-office box. He lived aboard in Newport and had a ring of keys that gave him access to dwellings more varied and mysterious than any I had ever seen. "I house-sit for people," he explained. Some of his people were away for years, he told me.

"Where are we living this week?" I would tease him.

My favorite was a Spanish hideout, more ornate than a wedding cake (Bugsy Siegel's place, I later learned).

Tony and I made love in strange beds and other, stranger places. He was endlessly inventive and I was a willing initiate. My fall—from grace, that is—involved massive four-posters, kitchen tables, kitchen sinks, bathtubs, front lawns, Spanish tiles, a staircase, the front seat, backseat and hood of Tony's roadster.

A leaf may have fallen in a canyon somewhere, but if it did, I didn't notice. I bobbed my hair, began dressing to show the figure I had and entertained the surprising notion that, like my cousin

Joannie, I was attractive for more than my money. In short, I was in love—and in a great deal of trouble.

My metamorphosis from titmouse to creature of the night did not go unnoticed by my father. "You look...good," he remarked to me at least once a week, never sounding pleased.

"It's the hair," I would tell him. "It's the dress...it's the tan, I went sailing."

"Mmmph," he would reply.

I was sailing—straight into the jaws of disaster. My cousin Joannie, undergoing a metamorphosis of her own into proper society wife, had a few words with me one Sunday, between chukkers out in the Palisades.

"You look good," she sniffed.

"I am good, evidently," I giggled. I knew the second the words were out that they were a mistake.

"Tony?"

"I see him occasionally."

"Oh, for God's sake. I told you when I introduced you. He's nobody serious."

"We'll see." Mistake number two.

"Your father would have a fit."

"Yes, if he knew."

"Great, Stan! Great!" For a dull man, Joannie's husband, Stan, was an exciting polo player. As he went thundering past, Joannie blew him a kiss.

"I'm happy," she told me. "I wish you the same someday. Stan makes me feel...safe, like he won't let me hurt myself anymore."

"That's wonderful." Joannie's version of happy sounded dreadful to me.

We were parked on the top of Mulholland Drive, in what they now call an "overlook"—because lovers were overlooked there,

I suppose. I was crying, sobbing really. Someone had blown the whistle on Tony's and my affair. Someone being my cousin Joannie, I surmised. My father wanted it *over*. "And now."

"I can't give you up," I wailed into Tony's damp shoulder.

"Sure you can. No worse than quitting nicotine sticks or hootch. No worse than heroin or any other vice."

"You are not a vice!"

"Sure I am." I'd ruffled his pride.

"Daddy says you're a gangster."

"He does, does he? Do you believe him?" I shook my head no, snuggling against costly cashmere. Tony handed me a French-milled handkerchief, monogrammed, like my father's.

"I want to show you something," he said. Below us, Los Angeles glittered to the sea. It was a clear, full-moon night. Catalina hulked in the distance—barely visible, like the Loch Ness monster. Tony took my hand and helped me from the car.

"Come look," he said. He stepped to the rear of the car, flicked open the trunk, pointed inside. "Look," he urged.

I am myopic, so I peered in obligingly, blind as a bat.

"What do you see?"

"Not much...I see...a body? No! Oh, thank God. A blanket!"

"Remind me not to call you for a witness."

Tony leaned past me and stirred the depths. He drew something up from the blanket's folds.

"A gun!"

"A machine gun." He cradled it like a baby in his arms.

"Now you think maybe I'm a gangster? That Spanish joint you're so fond of is Bugsy Siegel's."

"If you're going to shoot that thing, I think you should take it north of town. There are noise ordinances around here."

Tony laughed, wrapped the gun back in its soft blanket, then hugged me.

"That's what I like about you," he said. "Nothing throws you.

Are you cold?"

I was shaking, but not from the cold. Tony was a gangster and I was in love with him.

"What'll it be?" he asked. "Vegas or Tijuana?"

Tony and I were married in Vegas with white roses, stephanotis and two hired witnesses. Somebody called the press.

MOGUL'S DAUGHTER WEDS MONSTER.

HEIRESS MARRIES MOB.

Was I the last to know? Evidently.

"We're famous, Tony," I laughed. We'd pulled up at a news-stand to read all about it.

"Infamous, baby. It's a little different."

Very different? I didn't think so. You'll see why when I tell you about my father. I suppose I left him out because no one else ever does. When I said I came from the Silver Spoon Set, I could have said the Silver Screen Set. My family is movie royalty. My father, like the Warner brothers and Mr. Cohn, had a movie studio. I grew up with the stars in my face, if not in my eyes. My birthday parties featured Edgar Bergen and performing ponies, poodles and friends. Judy Garland sang "Over the Rainbow." Mickey Rooney danced. My father spent these parties promising me I'd have a life "away from all this"—as though the glitter and the glitz were some glamorous gutter. Maybe for him it was.

"Make what you know," the movie adage has it, and my father's studio made gangster films. Now, they say all studios have their underworld ties and my father's was no exception, although his ties may have been exceptionally close. Of course, my mother and I were shielded from all that. Of course, eventually, we found out.

What I didn't know, when I up and married Tony, was that my father opposed him not just because he was a gangster, but because he was the wrong gangster. I was marrying into a rival family from the one my father had ties to. This wasn't the kind of thing he'd explain to me. Like a Mafia chieftain, he needed to make no explanation of his whims. He gave an order and expected to be obeyed. I disobeyed him.

"We may have screwed up, baby," Tony told me when I told him this. We were on our honeymoon, shacked up together in a romantic mountain cabin. No phones. No fuss. Screwed up? I couldn't see it. I was in bliss. After Vegas, and those headlines, we drove south and east to the Grand Canyon. Tony had a friend with a cabin.

"We'll just have a good time until the fuss dies down," Tony told me.

We settled in to chop wood, carry water, make love. After a week, I was chopped, chapped, carried, happy and slightly bored. We'd seen woodpeckers, ravens, hawks, crows. We'd seen coyote, deer, elk, and even a bear. We'd made love. We'd made pancakes, fried eggs, steaks, beans and more pancakes. I wanted to go to town.

"What for? You've got to cycle down in a situation like this. Learn to appreciate the little things. A good cloud...that's an event. You get used to waiting. You stop waiting eventually."

"Are we talking jail time or Surrealism?" I asked.

Tony laughed. "A little bit of both...We can't leave, baby."

"Can't? I'll walk out if I have to."

Tony took my hand, kissed my palm, ran his tongue all the way up my underarm. I didn't want to leave any longer.

"I wasn't supposed to marry you," he said.

"Daddy'll get over it."

"Daddy's not the problem."

"Yes, he is. At least, for me."

"He's half of it, then."

While the piñon logs crackled merrily and our pinto beans simmered, Tony confessed to his life of crime. I lay with my head on his stomach. His penis nestled in my curls. I felt completely content. What was a little numbers-running between friends? That was back in New York. A little jail time? That was behind him. What did any of that have to do with Tony and me?

"This is a good story," I told him.

And it was. Hell's Kitchen to Hell Raiser. Hell Raiser to "Fund Raiser," a catchy euphemism for numbers collector, a petty mobster on his way up. Until he was brought down. Then jail time, as a favor to his boss, and now freedom. Freedom and me. I liked it. In a sense, I'd escaped my father's jail too.

"So, what were you doing in California?"

"I was on the lam."

"In Newport?...What were you doing really?"

"The guy I worked for thought I should try to break into show business."

Tony paused. His stomach rumbled ominously. Beans or nerves? He was leveling with me.

"Go on. How were you supposed to break in?"

Silence. Not even a stomach rumble. And then the *thump* of a fresh load of snow landing on the cabin roof from the shifting fir trees.

"Tony?..."

"Hmm?"

"Do you sing or act or dance...or?"

"Or are you my break into show business?"

I already knew. I just had a few simple questions.

"How much trouble was she in?"

"She?"

"C'mon. My cousin set this up. How much trouble was she in?"

Tony sat up. Now he cradled my head in his lap and stroked my forehead—fondly, I thought.

"You're good at this," he said. "You figure things out."

"Of course I do. A studio's just like a small country. I grew up listening to my father defend his dictatorship against all comers. That's quite an education."

"Right, so how'd I slip by?"

"You kissed me. Let's go back to how you were going to blackmail my cousin and ruin her chances of marrying the Dork."

"Bingo. You're good at this."

"So, my cousin set me up, I fell for you—"

"Right."

"And here we are."

"Right. Now let's go back to how you slipped by," Tony cajoled. "You were supposed to be a mark."

I sat up now. The fire was getting low and needed another log. I pulled on my French peignoir, knotted my hair into a loose chignon and anchored it with a tortoise pin. I crossed to the cabin door, opened it to the gusting snowflakes and snagged three logs from the cord outside the door. In one week, we'd put quite a dent in it. In two weeks, we would need to start chopping more. I had not yet learned to love an ax. Tony, shivering under the covers, grinned at me.

"Close the door, beautiful. What are you thinking about?"

"Heat," I lied. I had married this man against my father's will. This man had married me under false pretenses, against his capo's will. I was angry.

"I only married you to get away from my father," I told him.

Tony gathered the blanket around him. I'd left the door ajar and was setting more logs inside, two at a time.

"What?"

"I said, I only married you to piss my father off. You were the mark."

Thump! More snow. And the wind was picking up. I hoped Tony was freezing his considerable balls off. I hoped—

"Is it true you only married me to piss your father off?" He sounded pretty miserable for a hard-boiled gangster.

I didn't answer. I was hard-boiled myself, thinking about cold, not heat. Could Tony be cold enough to have married me as his show-business break? Or just to piss off his boss?

"Hey, you're going to freeze my nuts off."

"Good." I slammed the door. I threw the logs at the fire. Tony huddled in his blanket and watched me.

"You're mad."

"You're Einstein."

"C'mon, get back in bed, baby."

"Not on your life."

"Don't say that. Don't use that expression."

That's when it hit me. Tony was scared. Really scared.

"Whose place is this?" I asked him.

He glanced away. My stomach flipped like a crepe.

"Not?..."

Yes. Our mountain hideaway was a mob hideout. Our honeymoon was really just a truce. At best we were sitting ducks. At worst we were dead ones.

"You should have been an actress," Tony said. "Your thoughts show on your face."

"Then, what am I thinking?"

"That we love each other."

"No way."

"That we're stupid."

"Maybe."

"That we love each other *and* we're stupid?"

"Yes."

I was my father's only daughter. His men would kill Tony. ("Get him, and get her out of there.") On his side, Tony was the beloved son that his gangster boss had never had. ("Eliminate the girl; get Tony out of there.")

"There" was not so much our hideout or even our marriage. It was proximity to my father's mob connections. Or, in my case, Tony's mob connections.

"I gotta tell you something," Tony told me. "I do love ya."

"Yeah. Me too."

"Get back in bed, then."

The fire was burning and so were we. There is something about imminent death that enlivens the senses. When I say we made love, I'm not sure that's accurate. The love may have already been there. What we made was the house I've lived in, lo these many years, the house of love. I climaxed first repeatedly. Then Tony. The fire crackled and roared.

"What are you thinking?" Tony asked.

"Look at my face. I can't think."

It was a good thing too.

The first bullet shattered the window, tore at the wall, silenced Tony mid-thought.

"So, don't," he was saying, until the next bullet sheared off the back of his head and he slumped toward me. I am told I started screaming and kept screaming until the next volley of bullets pierced my neck, shearing my vocal cords, all but severing my spine.

While I hovered up by the ceiling and my body rode below me on the hospital gurney, I learned we were the victims of a mob hit—in fact, two of them. One for Tony. One for me. I learned this from the two consiglieri negotiating the hospital corridor, calling it "tragedy" and "even." Calling it "quits," to avoid further blood-shed. Of course, they couldn't know I was listening. At the time, I was, in their words, "as good as dead."

The truth is, I was one better. *Happy*, until the doctors yanked me back.

I don't know how my father feels about what was done. He's never brought himself to see me. I cannot speak, so I don't complain. I cannot feel much physically, so what I do is remember. I remember Tony loved me. I remember I loved him. We dreamed of a life together. I remember that too. In a sense, that is the life I've had. The last thing my body felt, since the bullet ended all feeling, was my lover's touch. As for Tony? I like to think that Tony died knowing I was stupid with love. Who could deny it?

Driving Through the Desert, Staring at the Stars

Casting Call

[WRITER DU JOUR] Armed with barbed-wire around a broken heart, she looks better than she feels. She's too young to be so old, and too old to be so young....LEAD (138)

DRIVING THROUGH THE DESERT, STARING AT THE STARS

By the time we met, he was in trouble. He'd been in trouble for years. I was there to write a movie—with him, not about him. I was young and a little dazzled. He was old, grizzled, famous. We both had broken hearts.

"Come as you are," the writer told me on the phone. "But come now, quickly, or I can't do this. I'll probably drink myself to death. Are you young and pretty?"

I was young and pretty. I was also self-destructive. How many times can you wake up in bed with a gun and tell yourself it's an accident?

"I'm young and pretty," I said.

"That will cheer me up," the writer promised. "Can you dance?"

I could dance.

"Come now. I'll send a plane. Come as you are."

One hour later, I met the plane near my mountain town. We winged toward the writer's desert hideaway. From the air, as we landed, the palm trees looked jaunty as poodle tails, the swimming pools were turquoise stones scattered across the desert floor.

A young man met my airplane, the writer's "nephew," he told me. I'd brought a typewriter, canvas shorts and a fear of snakes. I was wearing a tank suit and a sarong skirt. "Come as you are."

It was mid-afternoon when I walked into the writer's hideaway. The sounds of winey, whiney conversation and dinnerware clattered across the saltillo tiles and met me at the door.

"Come in, come in," the writer cajoled. "She's here!" he explained gaily to his luncheon guests. "The most talented young writer in the country!...And so pretty!"

Maybe it was the introduction. I stumbled entering the sunken room.

A dozen heads swiveled to watch my entrance, a pratfall.

"Don't fall for me," the writer laughed. "I'd break your heart." "That's been done by experts," I shot back. "The smiling woman before you is a fraud."

"Ooooh! Goody! I love frauds! Sit by me," the writer demanded. He patted a suddenly emptied chair—the nephew's.

"Sit by him, honey," an older woman crackled. I shot her a glance. She closely resembled a lizard: alligator skin, beady eyes, too many years in the sun. "He doesn't bite—anymore. He may not even chew."

"Ethel, what a mean thing to say," the man beside her chided. He too was tanned, reptilian, glitter-eyed. "I'm his doctor," he explained with a nod at the famous writer.

"I've been drinking," Ethel volunteered. "Sit by him, honey. He's really very nice."

"No matter what you've heard to the contrary," the writer chipped in, taking my hand and pulling me to him.

"Nothing," I said, slipping beside him, kissing his cheek.

"What a disappointment?"

"The kiss?"

"Kisses are never disappointing. People are," he said.

It was three P.M. The desert sun blazed its hottest, a hundred and twenty degrees. Plus. Not even chilled Corvo could deflect its blows. The luncheon withered like a plant left in the sun. The writer retired for a siesta, staggering slightly.

Staggering slightly myself, I elbowed open the sliding door and lugged my typewriter poolside.

"You'll burn!" the nephew warned me.

"In hell?" I asked hopefully.

The nephew was standard-issue gorgeous: perfect teeth, perfect tan, perfect body. A better body than Santini, the man

I was getting over.

"You're staring," the young man told me. "I'm taken."

"Oh, hell. Don't let it flatter you. I'm just horny. My lover left me for an older woman. He claims I wore him out."

"Touché," the nephew answered. "Ring Alma if you need anything. Alma is the live-in peasant."

"Charming."

"Yes, I am," he replied. "But only to them that counts."

I wasn't about to get into it. I pulled down my sun shade, pulled down my top and turned my lust to the sun. I heard the patio door slide shut and knew I was alone. I was there to write a movie, not get laid. The famous writer knew a lot about the Mafia, about the secret life of J. Edgar Hoover, about everything—or everybody. I was supposed to help him get it on the page. Not likely, if you asked me.

Jesus! What a catastrophe! The writer had ended lunch out on his feet. He started slurring and repeating himself an hour before that.

"You can't mix the pills, darling," Ethel had warned.

"Sure he can," the man beside her, the doctor, riposted. "I'm his doctor."

"Then fix my fucking heart," the writer snarled. "Darling."

The doctor and Ethel laughed nervously.

"They're killing you," I whispered in the writer's ear.

"From the mouths of babes," the writer whispered back. Under the table he grabbed my hand. His was cold with sweat.

"*Té, señorita?*"

Had the door slid open? I covered my chest, squinted from under my shade. Alma—I assumed it was Alma, small, dark, stern as a Mayan carving—stood inches from me.

"*Alma?*"

"*Sí.*"

"*No té, Alma. Agua. No. No, margarita.*"

"*Tiene dolor?*"

"Of course I *tiene*—I mean, *tengo*—*dolor*. Why else would I be drinking in mid-afternoon?"

Alma smiled thinly. "*Yo no sé, señorita.*"

She didn't know and I wasn't about to tell her. The woman Santini had left me for—Caterina, there's a name—was the same height as Alma, small, feisty, muscular, scrappy—like a Jack Russell terrier, the perfect Mafia wife. Genetics conquers all. Alma reminded me of Caterina—everything did. Alma made no move to get me my margarita. I snatched up my towel and stalked into the house.

"It's not easy—being young and beautiful and talented."

The writer whispered this sweet something into my ear. We were dancing together to the club mix of a popular Bee Gees song. The mix was vaguely Latin. So were the writer's dance steps. I followed him with ease and amusement. He was a witty dancer. So was I.

"Anyone ever tell you you dance like an angel?" he asked.

"A fallen angel."

"Good God. I love a clever woman. As long as she's beautiful too."

It must have been true. We'd been dancing together over an hour while the nephew fumed at the bar and glared bullets in our direction.

"He's boring," the writer giggled, catching my glance. "An *amour fou.*"

"Aren't they all? He's very pretty. Prettier than I am."

"Can you kiss?" the writer asked hopefully. "He's a boring kisser."

We touched tongues. Out of the corner of my eye, I saw the nephew turn away in a huff. Another glorious young man, standing right next to him, signaled the bartender to buy him a round.

The writer's tongue was soft, quick and sweet. Santini's had tasted of cigars. I licked the writer's lip. Tiny pebbles of salt clung to them from our margaritas.

"Salty," I said.

"The good things always are," he advised me. "Come here. Let me lick your back."

It had been years since I'd kissed like we did then. When had kissing become a lost art, something you did before the main event?

"Don't sleep with me," the writer said.

"I don't want to," I told him. "I want to kiss and dance."

We did that for two more hours. We did that even though the young man left us—left us touching tongues, exploring teeth, twined together and sighing.

Top down on the writer's convertible, holding hands, we drove home through the desert, under stars bright as diamonds, studs in a black velvet night more gaudy than anything Harry Winston might concoct. We pulled off the road once, to tango amid the sagebrush, alert for sidewinders, dancing to the scratchy sound of a Spanish station coming in tinny from across the border.

The writer had cancer. That, and heart trouble. They'd operated on the cancer. They'd operated on the heart.

"It was a valve, they said," the writer told me. "What do they know?"

We were poolside together the next morning. We were in the lull before the writer's entourage arrived. The sun was still climbing toward its furnace glow.

"So what happened to you, really?" the writer asked me. We were holding hands again.

"He left me for an older woman. Italian."

"Wanted a mommy? Those Mafia guys all do."

"Who knows? He wanted to break my fucking heart."

"Mine's married," the writer told me after a long moment. "They always are."

He released my hand and slid into the pool. I turned on my side and watched him paddle—not quite a breaststroke, not quite a crawl. A strangely syncopated dog paddle.

"You're an original," I teased him.

"We're both clichés," he shot back. "Maybe that's why I can't write about it—him. I write about everything else."

We both knew that "everything" did not include my assignment.

"Will you write about kissing me?" I asked him.

"If I live long enough."

"And if you don't?"

"Then you'll do it for me."

"What would you like me to say?"

"Oh, that I kissed even better than I wrote. That anyone who didn't love me was a fool."

I left the next day. The writer was drinking heavily. If I'd stayed, we'd have had adjoining berths on the *Titanic*. I told him that and kissed him good-bye. It was a sweet kiss, perhaps our best.

"Good for you," he told me. "And keep our bargain."

I'm ashamed to say that it has taken me all these years.

He kissed better than he wrote. Anyone who didn't love him was a fool.

THE RUIN

Casting Call

[MR. & MRS.] A husband and wife married to their marathon marriage as much as they are to each other. He's got a gourmand's bloated decadence; she began as a dish and ended up with a sour taste in her mouth....LEADS (146)

THE RUIN

I am a creative genius. You can believe me or read my reviews. Myself, I read the reviews. I read them a lot, now that I have time on my hands, cooling my heels in the Roman hills. Like Napoleon at Elba, I am in exile. Exile, not decline. No matter what the critics say. No matter what the studio heads concur. My powers are *not* waning, although my popularity has. For the moment, anyway.

"You'll make a comeback," my wife tells me. Her genius for the right thing to say is probably the secret to our marathon marriage.

In the meanwhile, before my comeback, we have rented this villa, at great expense. (I make a considerable income off video rentals of my early films.) I call it a villa—everyone does—but it's actually down at the heels, just like me. Once it must have been glorious, parts of it still are. My wife likes the olive grove. She spends mornings and early evenings there, tapping away at her laptop. A novel, this time. Unless I'm mistaken, it will be a novel about a creative genius and his long-suffering wife. There seems to be a special niche in New York publishing for these plaints. I say artists bent on marrying should enter the matrimonial state at their own risk. Maybe a simple inscription, a banner, should be held above the bride and groom: *Abandon all privacy ye who enter here.*

To date, I have had seven books written about me. Several by my wife—detailing our marital adventures under the guise of arts coverage—and several more by others, all of them women, one of them a former mistress. And yet, despite my celebrity, my career is in eclipse—overshadowed by personal notoriety, I'm sad to say.

"Not sad enough," my wife remarked recently. This was uncharacteristically acerbic. Olive grove and novel notwithstanding,

I think she finds our exile difficult. She may even be lonely—
despite the constant stream of visitors who make their way to our
villa door. Ignore what you may have read. I have never been
more sought out.

*Don't let him fool you. It's bad enough that he fools himself. My hus-
band has a particular genius for self-deception. Do I sound bitter? I'm
merely reporting the facts. The facts are these: We have fled America to
the more forgiving clime of Rome.*

*My husband would have you believe that his debacle was a fabrica-
tion, that the subsequent charges were a witch hunt, that we moved here
merely to sit out a shift in the critical winds. Nonsense. We got out of the
country one step ahead of the law with a fourteen-year-old actress and her
mother crying "Rape." Rightly so, I think. That's right. As incredible as
it may sound in light of my husband's and my long and tangled marital
history, and my own highly publicized, highly self-aggrandizing martyr-
dom, I side with the girl. Maria. Genius must be served, but I draw the
line at Maria. It's hard, even now, to say her name.*

*Maria di Casio was a talent that came along once in a decade. My
husband knew it. Maria herself knew it. Most of all, Maria's mother
knew it. Her daughter was her ticket and she planned to cash it in.*

*"I'm going to cast a local," my husband told me, until he met Maria.
She came to her audition in downtown Manhattan dressed as a Sicilian
bride. What a vision, the dark-eyed girl in white, passing through the
turnstiles of the 34th Street subway exit, like Persephone wandering the
halls of Hades.*

*"She's it," my husband breathed. "She's perfect," when Maria made
her audition. He has an unerring eye for talent, and Maria was no slouch
either. No singsong, that's amore amateur. Not this girl. Unlike the many
pizza pie readings before her, Maria's accent was authentic Sicilian,
sharp, clipped, guttural and secretive.*

"She's perfect," my husband told me—and, for once, I had to agree.

Like many directors these days, my husband conducts his casting sessions with the aid of a videotape. Given all the caveats about video being a different medium from film, you can still tell a great deal. As a rule, my husband erases the tape once he's viewed it. This time, he brought the tape of Maria home.

What do you need to know? That in nuance and shading she matched the premiere American actor of our time, who had agreed to read with her since they would be working together? That she was not only beautiful but timeless in her beauty? A child, a woman and all women? Even on videotape, Maria was a revelation. She made all the other contenders seem mannered, trite, modern. No question, my husband had to have her.

I'll bring it up myself, that imbroglio with the girl. Much as I detest it, it has to be dealt with. Even my wife says that. Personally, I don't see what all the posturing is about. I'm not the first middle-aged man to do what I did. And she's not as young as she says. The day I cast her, explaining that some of the scenes would be explicit, her mother assured me she was eighteen. Not that eighteen is exactly doddering, but it is legal. The whole thing strikes me as a technicality. A witch hunt. If that sounds defensive—well, you haven't met the mother.

In fairness to my husband, I should talk about Maria's mother. Now, I'm a feminist and I certainly like and trust other women, but Maria's mother? Her name was Randee, her spelling, not mine, and you've met women like her. She's my age, but she looks thirty-five. Slim-hipped, boyish, angular. I admired her eyebrows—fierce black lines—and the jut of her cheekbones. She was distinctive, attractive in her way, and she used it.

The day I met her, a week after her daughter was cast, she was waiting in the hall outside the rehearsal space, wearing blue jeans and a black silk blouse open to the waist. She was reading. Neruda, I remember.

I'm surprised I remember. What I noticed, what anyone would have noticed, were her breasts—small, high, round, with brown nipples, dark and erect.

"Excuse me." I introduced myself. "I'm sure you didn't realize your blouse is unbuttoned."

"Really?" Randee looked up at me, laughing. "Thank God, I've got nothing to hide except these little things." She fastened a button or two near her waist. I found myself blushing—not for her, for me. Suddenly, my considerable bosom felt matronly, oversize.

"I'm Randee, Maria's mother," she said. "I know who you are."

"Are you comfortable out here?" My husband's normally thoughtful crew had provided her with a single straight-backed chair.

"Anything's fine for me," Randee said. "I don't want to disturb their work." As with the breasts, I felt suddenly bourgeois—worried about comfort? We were talking about art.

"Your husband's quite a presence," Randee volunteered, out of nowhere it seemed to me.

"Yes, well, I suppose he is, but I'm used to it." Did she mean he was sexy? I thought she did.

"I'll tell one of the A.D.s to check on you," I said. "To make sure you are comfortable."

"It would be nice to have water at least."

"I'm sure it would."

With that, I slipped into the rehearsal hall, nerve ends jangling. Were her legs broken? Didn't she see the water fountain just down the hall? Who, exactly, sentenced her to an eight-hour day in a straight-backed chair? Something was awry.

Maria's mother, Randee. That's what I was talking about.

My wife didn't like her from the beginning. At first, I didn't make much of this aversion. Randee was an attractive woman—attractive to me, anyhow—and that in itself could get my wife's nerves on edge. Not without reason, you understand. I've had my dalliances.

I read somewhere that prepotent sexual energy is a secondary characteristic of great statesmen, and a director is nothing if not a statesman.

So, yes, I've had my mistresses. I'm sure that doesn't surprise you. By now it doesn't surprise my wife either. Location romances are an occupational hazard in our business—or a perk, depending on your point of view. I heard her once describing my mistresses to a friend, and these were her words: "An occupational hazard, like dysentery when you're traveling in Mexico or India."

My wife and I had traveled to both Mexico and India. I acquired both dysentery and mistresses on each location. My wife waited impatiently for the fevers to pass. But I was talking about Maria's mother. Mistress material if I ever met it. Unfortunately, my wife met her too.

"There's a darling little martyr sitting in the hallway with her tits hanging out," she told me. "You might want to do something for her—I hope not."

"What's the problem?"

"She says she's *thirsty*." My wife's tone said "thirsty" was a metaphor for what ailed her.

Over the years, I've come to know and respect my wife's radar. She has an uncanny talent for detecting my attractions. In this case, she was a dowsing wand. Maria's mother was my type. I didn't mind her going to Sicily with us. It saved my trolling through the natives, a risky prospect in Palermo.

He didn't have to fuck Maria's mother, if you asked me. Did anyone? No. No, of course not. The crew did what the crews always do, close ranks around the director and his secrets—as if I wouldn't know. How could I miss it?

Its immediate effects were catastrophic. Poor Maria began having trouble with her lines. Of course, this meant muffed takes, elongated shooting days, concern about budget. Above all, it meant prolonged in-trailer conferences between my husband and Maria's mother as they conspired together to remove her block.

As you most certainly know, Maria, an Italian-American, was playing Maria, the Sicilian virgin, the love interest of the young mafioso thug my husband glorifies in the film. According to the script, she would be raped, abandoned and made a star. A lot of starlets could relate to that game plan. Everyone, and I mean everyone, wanted the part.

Hers was to be a brief but brutal part: betrothed to a rising mafioso, brutally bedded by another and abandoned by both. That's one scene of luminous vulnerability. One scene of ravaged innocence. One scene of womanly loss. Abracadabra: A star is born. What would be simpler?

As it turned out, almost anything.

My husband's movie sets are known for their catastrophes—heart attack, stroke, bouts of malaria, divorce, attempted suicide. No, I don't hold him responsible, but he certainly is the scene of the crime. What I do hold him responsible for is what happened to Maria.

The trouble began with a routine disaster—routine for my husband's films. The actor playing mafioso #2, the one who rapes Maria, was shot by his actress girlfriend. It was an accident—just read our press releases—and the actor would be fine. Meanwhile, his right arm was shattered and he was temporarily out of the running as a credible rapist.

"I'll play the part myself," my husband announced. It wasn't the first time he'd thrust a family member into a big role. I myself have played Mafia wives, mothers and girlfriends. While in their strollers, our children have done their bit too. "Crawl-ons," we joked. Now they're at school. "Anything for the movie" was practically a family motto.

I'm not faulting him for this. Most directors are exactly the same— real directors, that is. When Scorsese lost a critical piece of casting during Taxi Driver, *he himself played the deranged obsessive who sits in the back of De Niro's cab and talks about shoving a Magnum up his wife's privates.*

To tell you the truth, I prefer my husband's playing a rapist to that. At least in theory.

"What I want to know is, what's wrong with the girlfriend? I'd have killed him dead." My husband was fuming over the shooting.

"Why?"

"He's fucking Maria's mother."

"He's not."

"I'm serious. She told me herself."

"Who told you? Maria's mother?"

"The girlfriend. She came to see me in the trailer."

"Before or after she shot him?"

"What does it matter?"

"Plotting."

He laughed over that, but my head was spinning. If mafioso #2, a second-banana actor, was fucking Maria's mother, then who was my husband fucking? I knew he was fucking somebody. He had all the symptoms—excessive concern for my feelings, my welfare, my boredom level and an air of general distraction.

"I'm watching the inner movie," he used to say. For years, I believed him. I attributed his characteristic distraction mid-filming to the burden of carrying the production in his head. Bitter experience—in the form of a script girl named Jeannie—taught me that what he carried in his head were porno movies.

"Steady as she goes," I cautioned my husband.

My point was that he was midway across a movie—and a movie is a rickety bridge across the chasm of chaos. "Keep the drama on the screen," I urged.

"Don't be so controlling," he told me—as if he were in any danger of being controlled. "Stay out of this. Go write your little novel. Make me the villain. Write about how unfair I am, how dictatorial, what a monster. Write about my temper, why don't you?"

I went back to my typewriter, just as directed. I did not write about my husband's temper. I wrote about his crooked penis instead. When I got *that out of my system, I wrote beautifully. I find having something unpleasant to avoid does wonders for my concentration.*

The little idiot took my advice and shot him. I wanted to kill her. Maria's mother, that is. Fucking me and fucking a second banana—an actor! I suppose I'm glad his girlfriend told me. Of course, she's grateful I cast her at all, even as a Sicilian whore. Of course I cast her. She was an actress who could really take direction. She actually did shoot him, just badly. Still, Maria's mother was the one I wanted to nail. Do you know what she said to me? Let me quote:

"I am not chattel. I am not property. I am a woman with free will, and if I choose to fuck another man and you can't handle it— that's your problem. You don't own me."

I hate lines like that. At least, I hate them coming from a woman. I was the director, for Chrissake. I needed respect on my set. She yelled this at me outside the trailer.

I would have killed her, but that was beneath my dignity. I reminded myself that I knew of at least one other set, where a woman writer from *Ms.* magazine slept with both the screenwriter and one of the producers. What was it with these feminists? Didn't they like the movies?

Maria's mother might provoke me, but I would not let her harm my film.

The day it happened—it being the alleged rape—my husband asked for a closed set and Maria asked for her mother. A virgin with limited sexual experience, she wanted the assurance of having her mother on the set. Yes, the sex was simulated sex, but it was still sex and outside the realm of her personal experience, as Maria herself told me. I believed her.

"Everything will be fine," I assured her. "My husband is good at this."

"Sex?" she squeaked.

"No, honey, making it look like sex. You just do what he tells you."
I would regret these words.

I drove to location with my husband that day. Ordinarily,
when on set drama rears its head, I steer clear, writing, exploring wher-
ever we are filming—museums, natural wonders, anything of interest
besides movies. Maybe it was a protective instinct on my part that took
me there that morning. Maybe it was my husband's casually dropped
suggestion that it might be nice to have me there since he was nearly
wrapped. We drove to location in companionable silence. The lemon-yel-
low light of that Sicilian morning lingers in my memory, tart and sharp.
"Want me on set?"
"No. No, that's okay. You can camp out in the trailer. Listen if you
want."
(The rumors you've heard are true. My husband bugs his sets. From
the electronically sophisticated trailer, I could eavesdrop on the Kremlin,
much less the set.)
"I'm not sure I want to hear you fucking another woman."
"It's acting," he protested.

They say that rape is a crime of power. So how could it have
been a rape? I ask you, what power would I feel the need to exer-
cise over a helpless teenage girl? It was the mother I was angry at.
Her mother, who sat on my set that day, with her slight derisive
smile. Her mother, who watched me with a slight narrowing of her
eyes, sizing me up, comparing. I didn't rape Maria that day. It was
her mother. Her mother upstaging me. Her mother threatening
my authority. Her mother, Randee. She was just within my sight
line—tight blue jeans, silk shirt gaping open to show those brown
little breasts. "Anything more than a mouthful is a waste," she
used to joke to me in bed. But now she was flirting with a stage-
hand and I was in bed with her daughter.
Lights, camera, action.

The rumors began immediately. Maria flew back to America, citing "nervous exhaustion." The rumors flew back with her. The tabloids had a field day. We went back to Los Angeles, briefly, for postproduction, but the rumors were a distracting buzz—like noise from an improperly blimped camera. Nothing was ever proved, but we left L.A. Some final post work was done in London.

I don't know what made me listen. I told myself it was boredom. What I heard was something my husband can deny and something a court can't prove. The footage, damaged in the lab, is inconclusive, and besides, all movie sex looks real. The sound tapes were unintelligible, muffled by the roar of an airplane overhead. What I heard, trying to focus on Italian Vogue, tuning in only mid-scene, was the unmistakable sound of my husband's angry thrusting. Then, the sharp cry of the virgin Maria and then her mother, Randee, sobbing, begging my husband to "Stop it, stop it!"

Of course, none of this ever happened, according to the studio. The loyalty of the crew held firm and nothing was ever proved. If a director is a dictator, a crew is his trusty cabinet. To betray the director is to commit high treason. And so, young Maria became a casualty of war. I alone, listening in my husband's trailer, graced with electronic ears of incredible acuity, heard the damning exchange.

Maria's mother: "Oh, my God. You ruined her!"

My husband, sotto voce: "You deserved it."

RABBIT'S FOOT

Casting Call

[KATIE] Our narrator had the courage of her evictions. She gave it up where others gave in. The first rule of magic is containment, she might tell you—then again, she might not....LEAD (158) POSSIBLE NUDITY

RABBIT'S FOOT

I ran into him on the plaza in Taos. I hadn't seen him in years, except on the movie screen. He looked older, smaller, more tired and very, very glamorous. That must have been left over from the movies. I had a hard time sorting my impressions and I must have been staring.

"June?" He stared back with the crinkly squint his eyes were famous for. "June? Is that you?"

"I suppose so, Boo," I answered, and finished lifting the box of groceries onto the back of my pickup.

"Let me help you."

"I've got it."

By then a little knot of people were staring. He was, after all, a very famous movie star and not Dennis Hopper (who had lived in Taos for years—his drinking years—and was referred to as "Dennis" or "Oh, Dennis").

"Let's go somewhere," he said. "Somewhere nobody knows us." This was impossible. He was a movie star and I lived in this small town and had for nine years.

"Ogelvie's is okay," I said. It was the bar with the veranda that overlooked the plaza. I never went there anymore. I didn't drink.

It was the height of the tourist season, and the stairway into Ogelvie's was crowded. My friend Jane was working the door.

"Oh, hi," she said, taking in me and the movie star. "Let me get you a table."

"Stardom has its perks," the movie star said to me.

"She's my friend," I told him, but if he heard me, he just kept moving, smiling slightly at the crowd as he moved through it, acknowledging the slanted eyes, the slightly excited grins.

"Thanks, Jane," I told her.

Jane signaled a busboy and pointed to a four-top table.

"But it's a four," he protested.

"It's okay," the movie star said. The table was in the corner of the veranda, half in sun, half in shade. A big striped umbrella let you take your choice.

"Still drinking Virgin Marys?"

It had been, what—nine and a half years. That's what. And he remembered my drink. Of course, he was famous for his memory. He routinely astounded people with the details of former meetings, the meals they took together.

That's because he keeps a diary, I remember thinking. Like Andy Warhol.

"Yes," I said. "Still Virgin Marys. This is Nuevo Méjico."

"Two Bloody Marys, one tequila, one virgin," he told the waiter, another friend, Peter.

"That's one tequila, one virgin?" Peter repeated.

"I'm the virgin," the movie star joked. This was notoriously untrue.

I'll call him Charles, as the world knows him.

"So," Charles said, "what have you been doing?"

Nine years, I was thinking. Nine and a half, Allie was nine.

"Oh, nothing," I said. "What have you been doing?"

Charles laughed as if that were the funniest thing he'd ever heard. "Movies," he said finally, in case I didn't know. Our drinks came.

"Eenie-meanie-miney-moe, I think it's this one," Peter said, setting a glass in front of me.

"It better be."

"You're not in A.A. or anything, are you?" Charles asked. Peter coughed. We were both in A.A. So was Jane. Taos was a tourist town, and the best-paying jobs involved tourist dollars and alcohol.

"Why do you ask?" I asked Charles. "Just because we drank like fish?"

"Katie, Katie, Katie. What a shrew you are. I always loved that, June Bug." That was his nickname for me.

"Will that be all?" Peter was hovering protectively.

"We're fine," I told him.

I met Charles on an interview. He was a bit player in an important movie. It was his big break. I was there to talk to the director. I was writing for a film magazine. The director was a famous man, big and brash. He scared Charles to death. I spent most of the first afternoon reassuring him.

"I'm going to be a star," he insisted to me when we met later that night for drinks, after the shooting was over, after I'd unreeled three tapes listening to the director at dinner and at dailies.

"He said the same thing," I told Charles. "Your director."

"He did?"

"Everybody's saying it."

"That's great. You're my rabbit's foot."

"Actually, I am a rabbit's foot. It's in my chart that I make the men I'm with famous."

"Really."

"Really."

"So make me famous."

I told Charles to shut up about being insecure. Not just with me, with everybody. I told him to develop an interest in jazz and only talk about that when being interviewed. I also suggested he move into the Chateau Marmont as soon as the movie ended and stay there until the film was released. The Chateau's star-studded associations would lend him some panache.

"Guilt by association," I told him. "I spell it *g-i-l-t*."

"I get it," Charles said. And he did. When the film opened, his interviews were gems of hipdom. His price went up and so did his stock. He was on his way.

The second time I met Charles, I was interviewing him for a small foreign-film periodical where I was a sometime contributor.

"You see," I told him. "You're a star."

"And you're my rabbit's foot."

"What a memory," I kidded him.

"I keep a diary," he confessed. "I write in tiny, tiny writing and lug the journals with me everywhere. Even here. I looked you up."

"Here" was an Indian burial ground in Kansas. Charles, under his new name, was starring in a film about Indians, directed by a very famous actor. Rumor had it Charles was his protégé. And, maybe, his lover.

"Write good things about me," Charles said.

"What kind of things?"

"Oh, you know, the usual. That I have beautiful eyes, perfect teeth, a perfect memory, something interesting like that."

To humor Charles, who was going to be a big star, I wrote the bit about the perfect memory. My piece became film history.

What I remember about that time with Charles was the night I went to dinner with him and the very famous actor, the more famous actor. Charles ordered everything the actor did—buffalo balls, all right. Elk steaks, okay. Fried green tomatoes, sure. He even held his fork the same way and ate with real gusto.

"Are you imitating me?" the actor asked.

"Yes," Charles said. "I'm a vegetarian." They both laughed over that.

"And who are you?" the famous actor asked me. "Other than Miss *Cahiers du Cinema*?"

"She's my rabbit's foot," Charles told him.

"Now, there's a part," the actor said.

The last time I saw Charles, before this time, he was a very famous actor and I was invited to the set because he trusted me. He trusted me because my boyfriend was his idol. Charles and the press were not getting on. There were nasty things about his temper and his latest girlfriend. He was spoiled, the story went. Fame had gone to his head. So had a lot of cocaine.

We were sitting in his trailer, an extravagant lair with an enlarged Japanese TV screen at the back so he could amuse himself with films during the long setups.

"You look terrible," I blurted out the minute I climbed up the stairs.

"You see?" He turned to someone I couldn't see. "That's why I asked her here. She's honest."

"You asked me here because you want some press," I informed him. "I'm not fooled and your nose is red. You've got a cocaine booger on one nostril."

"Shit!" Charles' hand flew to his nose.

"What's it to you?" His famous costar stepped from the shadows. She was half crocked and surly. She was also married to someone else. Charles introduced us even though I knew her name and she didn't care about mine.

"What are you doing?" I asked Charles, meaning the cocaine.

"I'm splitting," the girlfriend announced. She stepped past me on the narrow stairs, jostling me with a famous breast. On purpose, I thought.

"If you write a word of this..." she hissed.

"A word of what?" I asked her. "You took the coke vial with you."

She glared at me then and Charles jumped up behind me.

"Let her go," I said.

I trust it was largely a matter of being in the right place at the wrong moment. The girlfriend closed the door after herself, and Charles went crazy. Before he was finished, the Japanese TV had a hole in its screen and an assistant director was pounding on the trailer door, telling him respectfully to cool it.

"Everything okay in there?" the A.D. kept yelling.

Clearly, it was not. I was hiding in the bathroom, with the door locked.

"Rabbit's Foot. You can come out now."

I'd flown in and was jet-lagged and more tired and amazed than upset by all the commotion.

"I'll just take a nap," I called back. "Let me know when your life's straightened out. By the way, she'll only dump you when the film's out."

"I've got Evian, "Charles replied, as if bottled water was the answer to everything.

Maybe it was. A generator blew and we were suddenly looking at a six-hour delay in shooting. I came out of the bathroom and Charles handed me an Evian on ice.

"Let's talk," he said.

"What's to talk about?" I asked him. "You're stoned, surly and getting bad press too. Because of the girlfriend, mainly."

"What should I do?"

"What do you mean what should you do? You should stop it."

"Your mouth to my ear, Rabbit's Foot. You should know."

Charles gestured to my hands, which were shaking.

"I'm fine," I told him. "I'm here to do a story and you're it. Not me and definitely not him."

"Him" was the famous actor I'd been seeing ever since that night at dinner when Charles had introduced me as his rabbit's foot. By the night in the trailer, the relationship was tearing apart in slow-motion pieces—like watching a snowslide take apart a mountain. That's why my hands were shaking. That, and the drinking.

"Rabbit's Foot," Charles told me. "We're falling apart. We have everything we ever wanted and it's killing us. All I ever wanted was to be famous and the love object of millions—and I am. I'm just not enjoying it."

"Wait a minute," I told him. "You may have what you wanted, but when I was a little girl I wanted a horse ranch, not a writing career. I planned to spend my days training horses and my nights counting the stars with someone I love."

"Sounds awful."

"To you maybe."

"Anyway, I don't see him settling in with your home on the range," Charles said. "Do you?"

"Where would all the fans be?" I asked. "Maybe you've got some tequila here?"

"Maybe I do, but the strongest thing you're going to get is a tequila Bloody Mary. I'm going to wean you off the sauce—and him."

"What will rehabilitating me do?"

"Improve my press, I hope."

That's how it started, the deal we made, and that's more or less how it ended up. I gave up booze and the famous actor. Charles gave up coke, temper tantrums and his costar. I don't know what everyone on the set thought we were doing the eight weeks—actually, I do. According to the tabloids, whose source was Charles' makeup man, Charles and I were having an affair, breaking the hearts of his costar and my famous actor. The rumors were juicy but they certainly weren't true—at least until our last night together.

I'd had six weeks off booze, even Bloody Marys, and six weeks off the actor. Charles had done his best work in years—the camera read his coke-free vulnerability as subtext. His "Monty Clift" fragility lent him pathos and power. Oscar time, they were talking, even before we wrapped.

We wrapped on a Friday night in Boise, Idaho. (This was another of Charles' neo-cowboy flicks.) The wrap party was a big barn dance at which Charles and I clung together because we were both shy without drugs. The press was there, and I still have a shot that ran in *People*. To be fair, the caption, *No Longer Alone on the Range?*, seems accurate, because we do look in love: a trick of the lens, I suppose.

If it weren't for the picture I wouldn't remember what I wore that night—Charles' black T-shirt over blue jeans duded up with a silver concho belt and some African beads. I would remember leaving the party, sneaking out early and going back to my rented hotel room. Where I gave Charles a copy of the story I was filing and we congratulated each other on our new, improved lives.

"What about that horse ranch?" he asked me.

"Oh, I'll get it. (Now that I'm sober.) What about the Oscar?"

"I'll get that too."

We made love, I think, because we surprised ourselves with our affection, with the way we really wished each other well.

"You know what this means, don't you?"

"I can't write about you anymore. I'd be compromised."

"No, that's what you used to be."

That's pretty much how we left it. The hotel room had clean white sheets and silly ranch-style furniture. Charles had skin that tasted of salt and cider vinegar. "Fish and chips," he joked when I told him.

"So what do you do out here, really?" Charles asked again. "I'd heard you were here."

"You really want to know? I ride horses and count the stars at night with someone I love."

"That sounds nice," Charles said. "Almost as nice as being rich and famous—almost."

He looked at me across the table then, with the one look I have never, in all his movies, seen him use to the lens. The look was clear as good water. You could see into it, to the very bottom. "I am what I am," the look said, "which may not be all that either of us would wish, but it is me."

I dropped my eyes before Charles did. As an actor, Charles had a thousand faces; the one he'd shown me was his own. Peekaboo, I'd said the first time I saw it. And that had been my name for him between us.

Jane comped us for our bill, and when Charles walked me back to my pickup, the plaza had emptied and we were finally alone.

"I wanted to tell you something," he said.

"And what would that be?"

"Thanks."

"For?"

"For everything. For keeping my secrets. I owe you a lot."

"That's mutual. More than you know."

"Oh, I doubt it."

I climbed into the pickup. Charles leaned on the running board and kissed me high on the cheek. I was surprised at the affection that washed over me.

"Let me know if there's ever anything I can do for you—or the kid." He stepped down.

What a nice guy, I drove off thinking, what a very nice guy. All right, I felt something more than that, but it was a quick stab, here and gone, beautiful and vanished, like a mountain trout.

I was eager to get home in time to meet Allie's school bus, in time to work with the green two-year-old I was so crazy about. After that, I wanted to get dinner, do dishes and count the stars.

I was in the middle of all that when the phone rang. It was Jane. She was just getting off shift.

"You're unbelievable," she wailed. "How do you know him?"

"Jane, c'mon. He's the father of my child—"

Jane didn't believe me. She thought I was kidding. No one knew, and if Charles would just stay away from small towns in New Mexico, no one ever would.

You might think I should have told Charles about Allie. I often thought that too, until that night. He had always known, I realized, in the quick, husbandly kiss at the pickup truck. But we had wanted different things and I was wise enough to let us have them. We had wanted different things and Charles was wise enough to let us go. If I had kept his secrets, he had kept mine.

HARRISON BOURKE

Casting Call

[CAT] With more highballs than high hopes, she has a razor wit—it's just that she keeps using it on herself....LEAD (170) POSSIBLE NUDITY.

HARRISON BOURKE

$\frown\smile\frown$

When I first met Harrison Bourke he was not yet Harrison Bourke, mogul of moguls. He wasn't even Harrison. Most people called him Harry.

I met Harry at a poolside party, not in Beverly Hills or Bel-Air, but in Bedford, New York, on Guard Hill Road, where my parents live. As a matter of fact, I met Harry at my parents' neighbors, the Howard Jappes. Mr. Jappes was, and still is, a Hollywood movie producer. He lived in Bedford because he hated Hollywood. Myself, I hated Mr. Jappes. I thought he was a snob, but he was a snob. Of course, so was my father—their snobbery made them friends—but at least my father had a sense of humor about it all. "All" being things like the perfect pool, the right cabanas—green and white striped—and the right guests—among them, Harrison Bourke.

"So," I asked Harrison when we were shoved together as the young people, "you're from L.A.; what are you doing here?"

"I'm on a buying trip," he replied, scanning the crowd over my shoulder, which annoyed me.

"Oh," I said. "You're in retail. With a name like Harry, what else?" I scanned the crowd over his shoulder.

"I'm buying writers," Harry said coolly. That stopped me.

"Writers?"

"Young, bright writers from East Coast schools, cocky, aggressive, well read, publishing a bit in small journals, hip magazines. Hungry writers with big appetites and a good learning curve."

"Pleased to meet you," I said. "So, you're an agent."

"Exactly."

"I'm the writer you're looking for—or one of them."

"What a surprise."

So, from the beginning, Harry and I had business together. I had just enough contacts and just enough moxie—not to mention talent—that I was right up his alley.

"Where are you published?" he asked.

"You should know," I told him. "Do your homework. Not all of us drop dead or wet our panties over Hollywood."

"Hollywood *money*," he corrected me.

"Hollywood money either," I corrected him loftily. "Bedford money is *money*."

I wince at that exchange. What a little snot I was, drawing the invisible line between art and commerce, kissing cousins really.

"So, where did you say you were published?"

"*New York* magazine—last week's cover, by the way—*The Village Voice, The Yale Lit* and, oh, yes, also *Ploughshares*."

"Nice list. Very writerly."

"Nice writer. What are you drinking?"

Harrison was drinking Perrier, not because he was a sober alcoholic—this was before the recovery movement got to Hollywood—but because he was actually working the party.

"So, what else is here?" he asked me, still scanning the crowd.

"What's in it for me?" I was drinking tequila, a bottle I brought myself.

"I'm William Morris West," Harrison offered.

"I don't sleep with my agent, my shrink, my father, or my priest," I countered.

"I can live with that," Harrison said. "You've got an agent."

I took his word and his arm, and made him my Hollywood agent.

"Let me introduce you to Riley," I suggested.

"Riley Moorecock? He's terrific."

"Why, you little sexist pig. You've done your homework on the Boys."

"We're talking Tinsel Town," Harry said. "A woman is hard to sell—as a writer."

I flashed him my tit—now you see it, now you don't. For an instant I thought, this man likes me. And not as a writer.

"Good," I said. "I'm sure you like a challenge."

With that, I led him over to Riley.

"Cat!" Riley greeted me. "Some dress." (It was red, slippery, minimal.)

"Some dress, some don't," I told him. "This is Harry Bourke, and the trouble with Harry is that he is a Hollywood agent who loves your work."

"Really?" Riley bit. His eyes came up dollars.

I left Harrison to close the deal and retired with my tequila to the far side of the patio.

"Who was that young man?" my mother came over to ask. "And what's that you're drinking?"

"Tequila."

"Is that a worm?"

"No, Mother. His name is Harry Bourke."

"Mmm. He reminds me of your father. Why don't you mingle?"

I did not respond. I was too staggered. My father was my father. Harrison was still someone named Harry. He might be my new agent, but that did not make him my daddy.

Just to prove it to myself, I doodled a little satire of Harrison on a cocktail napkin. *Prince Charming*, I labeled it. Harrison did look just a little like my father, but he was speaking into a megaphone of his grand plans. My father would never do that. My father—

My father stopped by the table and tousled my hair.

"Your young man desert you, sweetie?"

"He is not my young man. His name is Harry Bourke. He's my agent. My new agent."

"Ah. Howard knows his father."

"Howard probably is his father." At this remark, my father's jaw twitched. He liked Howard Jappes, remember. And my father was nothing if not loyal to his friends.

"You know, young lady—"

"Is this the temperance lecture?"

My father's face softened again.

"Sometimes, honey, you're just so—"

He broke off, letting it drop.

"So what?" I challenged. I was tipsy.

"Brittle—brittle and somehow self-regarding."

"Touché." I tilted my glass. "Sounds like you've been talking to Mother. She thinks I should write children's books instead of play with those nasty boys."

"I believe your mother suggested 'illustrate.' She thinks you have a talent."

"Well, I do."

"Beyond a shadow of a doubt." My father bent and kissed my brow, wincing slightly. "Think I'll do what your mother says and go mingle."

After signing up all of my best friends—we were rising literary stars, every one—Harrison came by to say good night. By then I was quite drunk, down to the worm in the bottle.

"Thank you," Harrison said. "You've given me quite a collection. I won't let you down."

"What are you? A worm?" (Not one of my better moments.)

I presented him with the cocktail napkin and, hoping for the charming looniness of Hepburn in *The Philadelphia Story*, I allowed him to escort me across the Jappes' back lawn to our back lawn, to a patio settee, where I put myself straight to bed.

The first year that Harrison Bourke was my agent I sold two movies to Paramount and took up skeet shooting at his suggestion. "You have to have something to do with that temper," he told me.

"What temper?"

"Trust me. Any girl who drinks like you has a temper."

"I have my bottle, you have your Sandy. Everyone has a safety net." Sandy was Harrison's girlfriend—good, solid Sandy.

A nurse, for Chrissake. At UCLA. Sandy was nice. Harrison was brilliant and abrasive and tortured by ambition. So unlike the rest of us. Sandy was his link to sanity. Sandy hated movies. They were frivolous, she said. Her ambition was to marry Harrison and have babies. Doubtless, they would all be brain surgeons.

The second year I was represented by Harrison, I moved on from margaritas to martinis. By then I was married to Michael Dowser, I would say *the* Michael Dowser, but his name has faded from public memory—just like his films. Michael, you may not remember, was a British director whose first American feature made fifty million dollars, big bucks in those days—very few of them mine. I was just the writer.

Harrison did not approve of my marriage to Michael. "It muddies things," he told me. It sure as hell did something. Married to Michael I went from a constantly employed writer to Mrs. Dowser. Harrison was not thrilled and neither was I. I drank about it.

"You want to work again? Get divorced. Nobody wants another director's wife as their writer."

This was back then and Harrison was right. When Michael and I got divorced—he went back to England, where he was "appreciated" for more than his "bucks" when his next film flopped—I was suddenly, gainfully employed again.

Harrison got me a job writing shoot-'em-ups. Action-adventure, we now respectfully call the genre. I was good at shoot-'em-ups. Mine were full of blood and guts and, yes, anger. I didn't write them under my own name, of course. I took a pseudonym, Peter Dicks. I thought the joke was obvious, but it went undetected. Unfortunately, so did I. Gobs of money and a gag rule were not my idea of a good time, but the money part wasn't bad. What rankled me was the anonymity.

"Make me a star," I begged Harrison as all the male clients I introduced him to became famous, more famous, and most famous.

"You are a star," he assured me.

"One with a name?"

"How about 'Twinkle'?"

It was Harrison who got me into Betty Ford. Since he couldn't drop my name, he dropped his. It worked because Harrison Bourke was nearly Harrison Bourke by then. He was locked in a power struggle with the incumbent president of his agency, the one he went to after William Morris.

"The old order and the new."

Harrison's new order involved something called "packaging," with which we have all become familiar. The object, lest we forget, was to put a quality film together "in house," right at the agency, and present the studios with a take-it-or-leave-it, prefabricated movie: star, director, producer and, yes, writer, lowly types like me.

The proximate cause of my last drink was Harrison's packaging of my best script with some folks I considered the dregs of his talent list.

"Harrison, you might as well throw it away! Think about it. My star's a notorious drunk. His work is sloppy. My director's a coke fiend, which guarantees the film will be over budget and never make its money back. My producer's the director's dealer and he knows less about movies than my mother. The whole project's a catastrophe. Start to finish."

To my surprise, Harrison agreed. "Right. What about you?"

"*Excuse me?*"

"You're a catastrophe. Who else will work with you? Or do you lay your failure to succeed at simple sexism?"

"Are you saying I'm a *drunk*, Harrison?"

"Lush is a nicer word."

"But yes?"

Harrison Bourke knows how to close a deal.

"I think you're right."

Harrison called Sandy to sit with me while he got on the phone to strike a deal with Betty Ford. Getting a slot in detox can be harder than getting a go picture, evidently.

Sandy arrived at my house—my community property from my divorce—and promptly started doing the dishes.

"What are you doing?" I demanded.

"The dishes. Someone has to. You'll be gone for months."

"Oh, God!"

Up until then, I'd been the brave little soldier—gay and cavalier. At Sandy's offhand prediction, I dissolved into tears. When Harrison arrived two hours later, I was still crying.

"Oh, Harrison," I sobbed.

"Thanks, hon," he told Sandy.

"Your dinner's defrosted, I'm going to the hospital, I'm subbing for Sue," Sandy told Hollywood's hottest agent. "Have fun, you two." Sandy left in a starchy sweep.

"What did that mean?"

"What?"

"'Have fun, you two.' Does she think I'm fucking you?"

"No. Are you?"

"Oh, Harrison. How chivalrous. But I don't fuck my agent, my priest, my shrink, my father, or my brother." He nodded curtly. Evidently not one of his favorite of my many jokes.

We were lugging my suitcase—Sandy packed it—to the Porsche.

"I've got another category for you," Harrison said. "For your list."

"What list?"

"The unfuckables."

"Okay, what?"

"Your A.A. sponsor."

"A.A.?" I squeaked. "Harrison, you don't really think I'm an alcoholic, do you?"

Silence.

Harrison knew how to protect a deal. Minutes later, we were spinning toward Betty Ford.

The less said about Betty Ford, the better. How about "It worked, I'm still sober." I prefer to focus on the drive through the desert, alone together, me and Harrison Bourke. Now, I recognize that the heightened, hallucinogenic aspect of the trip might have been, at least partially, chemically induced. Harrison was right, I was a lush. Add to that pill-head and recreational coke freak to the tune of a gram a day. Driving through the desert, call it detox, withdrawal or delirium tremens, Harrison Bourke, abruptly, looked very, very attractive to me.

"My hero."

"No, your agent," he corrected me.

I remember we had a half moon in the nighttime sky, a moon just as dangerous as Janis Joplin ever told us; Harrison, standard-issue *GQ* attractive, suddenly looked truly handsome to me.

"What are you staring at?" he asked.

"Am I?"

"You're not that stoned."

"All right. You look handsome."

"I am handsome. Spare me the drama, save it for the page."

I shut up after that, but Harrison did not get any worse looking. For one thing, he's a fast, smooth and confident driver. Safe, but not slow. He reminded me of my father.

"Chloe," I suddenly said out loud.

"Now what?"

"I'm naming our children."

"Stop it. I warned you once."

I was quiet after that. Harrison drove quickly and efficiently, passing with such celebrated aggression that you always felt a sense of victory.

Yes. They were expecting me. Admittance went with insulting speed and Harrison held my left hand while I filled out forms with my shaky right. "That about does it," the nurse announced.

"Take care of yourself," Harrison said, squeezed my hand and then left.

The crescent moon outside my window looked like an empty champagne glass. The palm trees were irritating as poodles' tails. The romance of the desert had disappeared with Harrison's Porsche.

I did my time at Betty Ford and I hated every minute of it. Sobriety was not my idea of a good time. I was nobody's good time either.

"Fuck yourself," I told my counselor when she suggested that my self-worth was shaky, that I thought writing was all that gave me value.

"I don't think you like yourself," she continued.

"Of course I don't," I told her. "I'm evidently a nasty drunk and so dishonest I couldn't admit it."

"Who could?" She gave me a beautiful smile.

"What?"

"I meant, me too. It's better now. You'll see."

It did get better. Not only for me, but for Harrison Bourke. During my first thirty days of sobriety, during the no-calls, no-visitors, no-fun phase of intense personal inventory, Harrison won the power struggle within the agency and was named President. He was ridiculously young and everyone predicted failure—just as they did about my sobriety.

My big concern was that I would not be able to write sober. Scotch got me past my censor, I always said. Imagine my surprise at finding out scotch was my censor, limiting me to a certain bleak and dramatized view of the world.

Sober, I couldn't stop writing, couldn't stop thinking all manner of interesting, previously unsuspected things. None of them vaguely resembling action and adventure movies. Nothing vaguely resembling life as I had known it. For one thing, I was cheerful. Every morning the sun rising over the snaggletooth mountains of Palm Springs gave me an undeniable pleasure. What would it be like, I wondered, to write something with a happy ending?

The day I graduated from Betty Ford, Harrison sent me a dozen red roses. I know that they were corny—"Classical," Dottie, my counselor, insisted—but I loved them.

I opened up the card—*Keep coming back*, signed *Harrison*. Where had he picked up the A.A. jargon?

"Remember, no emotional involvements for your first year," Dottie warned.

"With Harrison?" I squeaked.

As it happened, I didn't even see Harrison my first year. I didn't see Hollywood, for that matter. I had been out of the clinic exactly one week when my mother phoned to say my father was in the hospital, a stroke, could I come home?

Could I do anything else? I phoned Harrison to tell him

my plans. After all, he was my agent. Even to my jangled ear, he sounded uncharacteristically empathetic about my news—or just plain blue.

"You don't sound so hot, Harrison," I told him.

"I've been offered a studio vice-presidency."

"Oh, my God. That's great, isn't it?"

"I'm holding out for top dog."

"Oh." Did I sound too relieved? He was my agent, after all.

"Sandy left me."

"She did?"

"For a brain surgeon. He does something she can believe in."

"Oh, Harrison. I'm sorry."

"So am I," he said wanly. "I believe in movies."

He sounded like a little boy.

Sober, I found Bedford, New York, a very pretty, very stultifying place—not that I expected otherwise, not that it mattered. What mattered was my father, who had lost the power of speech and the use of his left side and required intensive physical therapy with slight promise of success. My mother was disconsolate.

The night I flew home, I found her poring over albums of their life together.

"You have no idea," she told me. "How persuasive your father was. He had no prospects—none—he grew up practically on the Bowery and now we have all this."

"All this" was Mother's phrase for Dad's considerable fortune, manifest all around her as ginger jars, cachepots, inlaid sideboards, Kardeshir hand-knotted rugs. Father's home was Mother's castle and she filled it with the spoils of war, the booty of his triumphant runs for C.E.O., chairman of the board, corporate king.

"It's not over, Mommy. Why don't you redo the TV room to surprise Dad when he comes home? I know you have been wanting to for ages." To her, Father was her life, now over, she feared. And so, I sent Mother shopping and I went to work with Dad.

My days rapidly took on a routine. Six A.M., wake-up call. Early-bird A.A. meeting. Breakfast at a greasy spoon—or what passed for one in Bedford—drive to the hospital for work with Dad. He couldn't read, so I clipped cartoons for him. One week, when *The New Yorker* was uncharacteristically dull, I sketched cartoons for him. Autobiographical cartoons featuring, da-dum, The Spoiled Princess. That was me, of course, rendered as some squiggly little lines and cartoon blurbs of my character defects. I drew the princess as she encountered real life, in exile from her true kingdom of life among the rich and famous in Hollywood. *Children?* I drew her thinking. *What are* those?

On a lark, I sent the strip to Harrison. It wasn't exactly a screenplay for him to sell, but it was something.

Love the comix, came Harrison's reply. *FYI. Children are an important part of your viewing audience. Harrison.*

I named my spoiled princess "Precious" and continued my chronicle of her spiritual growth. Precious faced the same dilemmas I did: life with mother, life without father, life without booze.

What's normal? I cartooned Precious thinking. *And why does it feel so abnormal?*

My mother shopped until she dropped and then, the feelings hit her. She curled up in a blanket in my father's den with the albums of their life together. Evenings, she studied them over a glass of sherry. Evenings, I spent attending a second, daily A.A. meeting. I talked about my mother's depression, my father's minuscule gains, the loss of my own life in Hollywood. It was slog, slog, slog. Once a week, sometimes more, I would call Harrison and moan.

"You sound fragile," he said once. "Maybe you should rent a comedy."

"Harrison!"

"Okay. Go to another meeting."

Well, I stayed sober. Harrison stayed President. His packaging ideas caught on and his power, whatever that really means, tripled. He was absorbed in his work. I was absorbed in my recovery, *very absorbed* in my recovery. A laugh riot of character defects and stale resentments, some of them marinated since grade school.

"Honey, why don't you rent some comedies?" an A.A. old-timer advised me. I was insulted. My taste in movies ran to things like *Throne of Blood* and *Dersu Uzala*, not exactly laugh fests.

"Rent them for your parents, anyway," Harrison directed me.

"No, tell you what, I'll send you stuff." He began FedExing videos.

And so, Mother and I enjoyed the new TV room. I would race home from the hospital, fix Mom dinner on a tray and leave her in the company of the Marx Brothers, Tracy and Hepburn, Cary Grant and someone, while I went to my evening A.A. meeting. After the meeting, I'd come home to find her smiling, curled like a kitty on the newly purchased couch.

"Time for bed," I'd tell her, and pack her off to a good night's sleep. Harrison's comedies were certainly cheering her up.

Not me. Withdrawal, stress, or both were giving me insomnia. I'd call Harrison to report in on the movie of the day. Most nights, I fell asleep on the new couch, waking when the sparrows started a racket in the forsythia bush just outside the window. Then a quick shower, a quick breakfast, early-bird A.A. and back to the hospital, where Dad watched the movie on his rented VCR and I flexed his limbs.

"I feel like I'm going to film school," I told Harrison.

"Well, you are," he volunteered.

Harrison had been successful with his packaging idea—so successful he was practically producing many of the films his agency packaged.

"After all, it's my recipe," he said. "How's your father?"

"He liked *Father of the Bride*...I think," I told him.

"You might want to try him on *State of the Union*," Harrison advised. Harrison had a weakness for Tracy-Hepburn films. He had us watching *Desk Set*, *Pat and Mike*, *Woman of the Year*.

"What is with you and Spencer Tracy?" I asked him.

"It's me and Hepburn. She reminds me of you."

"Oh, Harrison."

When I repeated this conversation to my mother, over fabric swatches for the proposed curtains, she said, "Mmm. He sounds like your father."

"How can he sound like Daddy? Daddy can't talk," I snapped.

For once, my mother laughed. Harrison's comedies were wreaking changes.

My mother and I have never had an easy relationship. It got easier over movies like *Holiday*, *Twentieth Century*, and *It Happened One Night*. I began racing home from my A.A. meetings to hear her reviews. One night, I got home to find Mom waiting with TV dinners for both of us. She'd waited on the film to watch it with me. Together we watched the drunken high jinks of *My Man Godfrey*. When it was over, Mom quietly stroked my hand.

"I'm so glad you don't drink anymore," she told me.

This was the first and only time my drinking was ever mentioned between us.

The day my father spoke his first words, Harrison phoned me at home as I walked in the door. I could not wait to tell him my good news.

"Daddy talked!" I blurted out. "He talked."

"That's great news," Harrison replied. "Just great. What did he say?"

"He said, 'Hi, Precious.'"

"Hi, Precious," Harrison echoed.

For once, I was rendered wordless.

"I've got some news too," Harrison told me. "I got offered

top dog."

"That's great! Are you going to take it?"

"If it's all right with you."

"What?"

"Look. Could you get away for a few days now that your dad's gaining?"

"Maybe."

"Meet me in Saint Louis."

Now that Harrison and I are married, I can't imagine not being married to him. It feels so normal that I don't understand why I didn't expect it from the very beginning. Harrison says he did.

"Well, if you did, it sure took you long enough to ask me."

"Not really. I'd have asked you sooner, but—"

"I was drunk?"

"It wasn't so much the drinking."

"What?"

"You were so brittle and self-regarding." Wasn't that the phrase Dad had used? It certainly was.

"What does *that* mean?"

Harrison laughed. "I don't know. Some New Yorker described you that way once—back when I was your agent. I used to know what he meant."

Harrison and I were tree-trimming as we talked. There are certain days, at certain angles, when Harrison does remind me of my father. But it's not so much his looks as his habits. They both make little stacks with their change when they take it out of their pockets. They both peel the crusts of their toast to sop up egg yolk. They both, stubbornly, eat too many eggs. Also, they both wind Christmas tree lights the same way, bottom up.

"Help me get the star right, would you?"

"I already did."

A Little Bit Of...

Casting Call

[HOMEOPATH] Our narrator is almost as tiny as the homeopathic remedies she dispenses. A keeper of serums and secrets, she works her magic behind the scenes....LEAD (186)

A LITTLE BIT OF...

In order to find me, you have to know what you're looking for. And you may not be looking for a four-foot-ten Chinese herbalist with a sideline in homeopathy. If you are, you can find me at the tag end of Melrose, sandwiched between a bicycle shop and a newly hip lamp store, specializing in Art Deco. I've been in the same place, too small and dark, for twenty years, although not spiritually, I hasten to add.

Hollywood "discovered" my practice when the agent Rosannah Leipsitz came to see me about her weight problem.

"I could gain weight on a lettuce leaf," she told me. "In fact, I have. I'm tired of being the butt of jokes. I can't even say the word *butt*," she sniffled.

I began gently to explain to her about the elements, about the way a body could be out of balance. Too much fire, for example, as was clearly her case.

"This is worse than astrology," she whined.

"And you are?" I asked.

"Virgo," she confessed. "I worry about everything and then I worry about it some more. It makes me good at contracts and bad at losing weight. When I worry I eat. Mango sorbet, that's my downfall this week."

"Too much fire," I observed.

"Too many clients," she snapped, and tossed her expensive mane of fiery hair. She did look like a dragon.

"What year?" I asked.

"Please. Nineteen fifty-two."

"You see? Fire. The year of dragon."

"I'll see fire, all right, if I don't do something about this weight before Oscar night. I've got a Bob Mackey gown and it's 'Mack' as in 'Mack truck,' believe me."

"You're a very beautiful woman."

"Yes, yes, if you like women, which they don't out here. They like boys with tits. Thank God I married a Brazilian. He's a Pisces."

"We do need water for balance."

"Why, when I can drown my sorrows in cold Chardonnay? Actually, I hate drinking. I only drink to keep my husband company. And since he's stopped, or I hope he has, I need to be at my best. And lately, I have not been at my best."

I had the distinct impression she was telling me about an affair. Some indiscretion which even in Hollywood had her embarrassed. Despite her bravura, I sensed an overlay of shame—deep shame.

"I wish there were a safe little pill," she said now. "Something you could take to erase your horrid childhood."

"Actually"—I spoke tentatively—"there is something you could do. Tiny little pellets."

"Like buckshot?"

"I suppose so." Outside the window a diaper truck rattled by. Rosannah spotted it and sighed.

"I'm the perfect agent," she said. "When one of my bastard clients ran off on his pregnant wife I gave her a year's diaper service for their daughter and invited her to all my A-list parties, hoping she'd shack up with someone else and teach him a good lesson."

"That's very generous of you."

"I'm a pushover, a softie, a cream puff. It's my deepest secret." The more she talked, the more certain I felt that further probing and investigation would confirm my initial, tentative diagnosis: Arsenica.

If homeopathy in general was a hard sell—few people could believe so little could do so much—a diagnosis like Arsenica was harder still. How could a deadly poison—even in minute amounts—be good for you, my clients wondered, and sometimes I wondered myself. But I'd seen miracles, and if she'd let me, I planned to work one for Rosannah Leipsitz.

"Let me take your case," I urged her.

"I thought you had."

"I mean formally. It would take two hours. There are a lot of questions, a lot of details."

"I'm good at details. I can find a loophole in a contract it would take a microscope to find."

"Well then, shall we set a time?"

"Tomorrow at five. I can say I'm meeting a client for drinks." With a toss of her hair, she was out the door, and not a moment too soon—a practice like mine flourishes in anonymity. I didn't want to set up shop on Beverly Drive and cater to the industry. I saw enough of the industry as it was.

"Are you home, sweetie?" Glennis' unmistakable voice preceded her into my shop. She came bearing gifts—a large bouquet of tiger lilies and an apricot net bag filled with Borghese products. Glennis liked to spoil me—"Out of gratitude," she said. And, I suppose, she was right to be grateful, although her case was routine for a Lilium Tigrinum, keynoted as hers clearly had been by a severe mental split between her sexuality and her spirituality. Untreated Lilium Tigrinums were the nymphomaniacs among us, those who spent three hours on their knees in church followed by three hours on their knees somewhere else.

"You look wonderful!" Glennis exclaimed, which wasn't true, but, nice to hear.

"I look like I always look, a wizened, wrinkled prune with slanty eyes."

"You're right about the slanty eyes," Glennis laughed.

"My neighbor just got hers with an overenthusiastic face-lift."

"Mine are natural. In my country, women have surgery to get eyes like yours."

Glennis' eyes were large, luminous pools—clear and tranquil since her successful treatment.

"You know what day it is?" she asked me sadly.

I did know. It was the second anniversary of Richmond Egley's untimely death. Richmond, of course, was Glennis' long-term lover, and it was he who had introduced Glennis to me, certain there had to be some cure for what he charitably called her "addiction," which another man might have seen, less charitably, as chronic infidelity.

"I lit a candle for him this morning," I told Glennis, nodding to the altar I had tucked on a shelf beneath my rows of remedies.

"Let's find a vase," Glennis asked. She trailed me to the back of the shop, where I reached beneath the bathroom sink for a cobalt-blue fluted vase that Richmond himself had given me in gratitude for my help with his smoking. We were filling the vase with water when the front door chimed and a woman's querulous voice demanded:

"Is there anyone *here*?" Even to my non-industry ears, the voice was familiar.

"Dear God, no," Glennis said. "It's—" She named a famous—or should I say infamous—movie star. "Could I slip out the back?" she asked.

"Of course." I unlatched the back door for Glennis while I caroled "Coming!" and headed for the front of the shop.

"Where were you?" my new customer demanded. She tossed back a veil of silvery-gold hair. "Is this your bag of Borghese," she demanded, "or did someone leave it here? I love this stuff."

"It's mine," I told her firmly, to her displeasure. "What can I do for you?"

"Well," she said, "I really think this sort of thing" she indicated my shop with a dismissive sweep of her multi-ringed hand—"this sort of thing is probably quackery. But I'm here. So we might as well talk about my situation."

"Would you like a chair?" I offered, motioning her to a needle-point rocker, which I believed to be especially soothing for a Platina like herself—a classic Platina. In layman's language, a real bitch.

Questioning would confirm—or alter—my intuitive diagnosis, but even I knew Her Majesty's reputation as a compulsive cheat, a true femme fatale filled with contempt for her many, mainly famous victims.

"First of all, I must insist on complete confidentiality. I've brought a letter of intent." Her jeweled hands popped open her Prada bag. She handed me a terse legal letter on the letterhead of a famed entertainment lawyer. The simple forbidding sentences swore me to confidentiality and nondisclosure, a security I afforded all my clients. I saw no harm in signing it, particularly since the lawyer who drafted the letter was an old and valued client himself.

"Do you mind if I light some incense?" I asked, not a liberty I'd have taken with an Arsenicum type, who might have been prone to asthma.

"Yes, yes, do what you have to to make yourself comfortable, and then make me comfortable, if you possibly can."

"That's what I'm here for."

I lit a stick of nag champa and poured each of us a glass of iced chamomile. The movie star accepted hers like she was reaching for an Oscar statuette.

"Thank you sooo much."

"Not at all. So, what or who brings you here?"

"We'll start with the who—my masseuse or my masseur, whatever the word is, he's a friend of yours?"

"Possibly."

"Confidentiality?"

"Could be. Why don't you just tell me in the simplest terms why you're here."

"That's simple. I'm a bitch. People say I am. Cold, overbearing, domineering, a diva. I call it acting."

"Other people call it 'acting out'?"

"Oh, probably," she growled. "Look, is it possible I could take something that might make me—" She paused and raised her arched brows even higher.

"You were saying?"

"Make me nicer, that's what I'm really saying. I've met someone I'd actually like to hold on to, my costar actually, in a new movie."

"We could try working together," I volunteered cautiously.

"Try? You're supposed to work miracles. Weren't you the one Glennis saw?"

I said nothing. I busied myself relighting the stick of incense, which had guttered out.

"Right. Confidentiality again. Well, if I thought I could really count on it—" She paused dramatically. I knew it was my cue to beg for her trust, but I left that leap to her. She didn't appreciate my reticence.

"Has anyone ever told you you're aloof?" she asked me. "Or patronizing? Or cold?"

A classic Platina, I thought to myself while answering with careful neutrality, "Homeopathy is a very precise science. I find it best to work with a minimum of emotionality, to keep the lens clear, so to speak."

"To keep the lens clear," she seized on my vaguely cinematic turn of phrase. "I'd like to be able to do that. So, what do we do?"

"I take your case. It's an intricate, precise and extensive set of questions. I weigh what you've said and come up with a diagnosis."

"And then I take some pellets or something? I've heard you use arsenic."

"In some cases."

"Not on me, I hope."

"Probably not."

"You can tell that already?"

The truth be known, I could tell that already, but not to her.

"Shall we arrange a time?" she asked after a long moment. She made the prospect sound like root canal.

"I could see you tomorrow, in the early afternoon."

"I'm on set."

"In the morning, the day after that?"

"I'm on set. Could we do this by phone from my dressing room?"

"We could, but not as effectively."

"Baby says this better work."

"Who's Baby?"

"Oh! It's just a pet name. Will this work?"

"If you're honest with me, and we get an accurate diagnosis, yes."

"Did-you-say-if-I'm-honest?" She got to her feet. Her tall, refreshing glass of iced chamomile hit me like a slap in the face. "*No* one talks to me like that," she concluded.

"I can see why not," I managed to joke, but her laughter, as she swept from the room, did not sound sympathetic.

"My God, what happened to you?" I looked up to see one of my favorite clients, the screenwriter wife of Harrison Bourke.

"I just had a close encounter of the weird kind," I told her, too professional to name names.

"But you're soaking wet."

"A refreshing glass of tea."

"And I thought I was the only one who drank like that," my client teased. "Give me a paper towel or something and I'll swab you off."

"They're in the back, right by the sink."

"Oh, goody. I love getting to snoop around."

Mrs. Harrison Bourke, although we all called her Cat, returned with a roll of paper towels and her best Florence Nightingale manner. She began to dab at me as I sat, still in shock from my baptism.

"Who did this to you?" she wanted to know.

"Occupational hazard," I replied. "I encountered a classic Platina."

"And in English?"

"A real bitch."

"I love it when you talk like that," she giggled. "I love it when you talk, period." She graced me with a girlish grin, and I smiled back with satisfaction. She had come to me as a true Natrum Muriaticum: grief-stricken, fragile, filled with self-loathing, plagued by difficult relationships with men, thin and dry-eyed, unable to cry out for help, except in terms a homeopath might hear.

"I'm a recovering alcoholic," she had told me. "I'm a recovering everything. I'm in love with a wonderful man and I'm afraid I'll botch it if I don't get a grip on myself. Can you help?"

I *had* helped, with 10M high-potency Nat. Mur., a single dose. It had worked like a charm.

"So, I'm really here for Harrison. He wants to stop smoking. I told him I thought you could help, and he said he was interested in stopping smoking, not starting voodoo. I'm wondering if you could give me anything. Maybe something that looks like vitamin C," she laughed.

"Let me think about it. Meanwhile, tell me, how are you?"

"I'm fine, Harrison's fine, Chloe's fine. I never thought I'd manage a sentence like that."

"You seem to be managing a lot of things."

"It's five years."

"Five years?"

"Since I've had a drink or a drug. My life today was unimaginable. It's so—spacious—I guess that's the word."

"You mean expansive?"

"That's what I came to talk to you about. I bought a building. A beautiful space, bright and sunny, half a mile from here, closer to the Strip. I thought I'd put a children's bookstore in one half and you in the other, if you're interested."

"My rent here is what I can afford."

"Then, what's your rent?"

"Why are you doing this? I mean, it's wonderful, and yes, I have wanted more space, but there are so many things, so many other things you could do."

"Sometimes what you need to do is say thank-you."

"I'll practice saying it now. Thank you."

With a quick kiss to my wrinkled forehead, Cat was out the door.

The next afternoon at five, when Rosannah Leipsitz darkened my door, I thought about the way it is with people, how someone like her could be called a shark or a barracuda and when you met them all that was forgotten. It was that way with her for me. We began the painstaking and delicate process of taking her case.

"How do you feel about doctors?" I asked her.

"They terrify me, and I should know. I see them all the time."

"Would you like a glass of iced tea?"

"What's in it? I'm terrified of being poisoned."

"Do you have a fear of dying?"

"Doesn't everybody?"

"On a scale of one to ten."

"Give me a nine point nine."

"Worse lately?"

"Yes, it's worse lately, that's why I'm here. It used to be asthma, and eczema. I hate dirt and germs. Now I'm afraid of AIDS."

"But someone like you, you practice safe sex."

"How safe can it be?"

"With proper precautions..."

"He was a gigolo. A bisexual gigolo. Why am I telling you this?"

"To get to the other side."

She laughed at that, thankfully. I noticed that she held her tea glass with the sleeve of her dress—a classic Arsenicum Album—anxious, fastidious and, yes, lovable.

I have been a homeopath for two decades. In that time, I've met no one who couldn't be helped by a little love and a little something else. I prescribed 15c Arsenicum Album daily for one month.

MOVIE PEOPLE

Casting Call

[EDITOR] With stacks of manuscripts piled on her bed, she confuses literary lady with spinster. In fact, she's edited herself right out of living.... LEAD (198) NUDITY IMPOSSIBLE.

MOVIE PEOPLE

I first met Peter over the transom, by mail. Three crisp, brightly written stories arrived. I liked them, admired their style but found their content repellent. They were stories about the movies, in my opinion an overrated art form drawing too much print as it was. People won't believe me now, when *tout* library New York wants to be in bed with the movies, but when I was coming up at the Magazine, it really wasn't done—and certainly not at the Magazine. Bad enough a writer like Pauline Kael—a real writer although people forget that since she writes about movies—had deigned to consider movies art. The rest of us did not need to follow suit. Short stories about movie people? In the Magazine? No. No, thank you. Without so much as a moment's thought, I fired Peter's stories back to him.

I had been working at the Magazine for nineteen years. Nineteen happy, productive, predictable years. I liked them that way. They had been that way ever since I graduated Wellesley and had been lucky enough to win an internship, which evolved, over time, into an editorial position, hard-won and cherished. I felt of my life at the Magazine much as I felt about my life at Wellesley; others might have chosen differently, but none better.

These are bright little things but lack the complexity and surprise we look for here at the Magazine, I wrote. I didn't give the rejection a second thought, even when the stories eddied in my consciousness for a few days, most notably throughout a long, halting, sweltering train ride to the Hamptons.

I had rented a summer house with my brother. It was an experiment—in fact, a two-part experiment. Part A, sharing with my brother, newly returned to the civilized world after two decades on the Coast. Part B, the Hamptons themselves. For twenty years I'd resisted the summer migration that found half of publishing buying fresh vegetables *en plein air* at the Farmers' Market in the Hamptons.

"Shake it up a little," my brother advised. He *would*. My brother, a Hollywood screenwriter from Greenwich, Connecticut, had shaken it up a lot.

"Not everyone wants life to resemble a milk shake, Wally."

"Live a little."

"I am living."

I summered, wintered, sprang and fell right at 15 Park Avenue, right my in beloved Murray Hill, beloved in part for being walking distance to the Magazine.

"Murray Hill. The Magazine. You call that a living?"

"It's my life, Walden."

"Thank God for that."

Walden and I were twins. Together, we had progressed from matching towheaded toddlers to bright blond young people to what we were now—wildly disparate adults. At eighteen, I entered Wellesley. At eighteen, Walden entered Yale, where he rapidly fell in with lower companions—movie people, or the children of movie people, who planned to be movie people themselves. The summer after our freshman year, instead of going to France with me, as promised, he went to NYU instead, to something called "boot camp." By August, he was armed and dangerous, invading everyone's privacy, insisting on shooting 16mm footage of private family gatherings with an ancient Bolex he'd acquired.

"You're a disgrace to your name," I told him when he intrusively filmed Mother running a gymkhana for the handicapped, a sort of Special Olympics on horseback.

"Nonsense," Wally snorted. He was named for Henry David Thoreau, who, as Wally pointed out, "did what he damned pleased."

"Maybe so. But..."

"I wouldn't hurl cultural aspersions if I were you, Miss Spinster-of-the-Year. You're following your namesake all too closely."

"Screw you, Wally." I was named for Emily Dickinson and preferred to keep my insults short and concise.

By the time I graduated *summa cum laude*, Wally had managed to drop out of Yale and air his ponyback Special Olympics on PBS. He crowed over the phone from L.A., "An Emmy nomination. And no one complained about invasion of privacy. They know they flop around like flour sacks. They're glad to be riding at all."

So there.

Spinster of the year? *Au contraire.* I considered myself a highly desirable item—just picky. I wasn't interested in the stream of look-up-my-sister-and-take-her-to-lunch strangers that Wally foisted on me my first years at the Magazine. My job was more interesting than any of them. For that matter, so was I.

"I'm coming home," Wally phoned to inform me. "I've rented a house for us in the Hamptons."

After two decades, this was news.

"I hate the Hamptons."

"Good. Nothing like a little healthy polarity. You love me, don't you?"

Yes.

Of course I loved Wally. I disapproved of him, loathed his friends, despised the way he made a living, but Wally? How could I not love Wally? He tried so hard to share his life with me.

The first year Wally was on the Coast, I got regular shipments of artichokes and avocados, two California specialties, if that fact had escaped you. *Castroville, Artichoke Capital of the World!* the crates bravely declared.

I was in my first apartment at 15 Park, the small one-bedroom.

I could not make guacamole, not to mention eat artichokes, fast enough to keep pace with Wally's shared enthusiasm.

After artichokes and avocados, we entered a citrus phrase. Grapefruit the size of soccer balls. Oranges like small planets. When I complained, Wally sent me a juicer and a piece of turf I belatedly learned was wheat grass, not a joke about New York.

We had a color-TV period, after his first Emmy. When he switched to features, I began expecting a screening room. Instead, he sent me jodhpurs, a crop and the collected Dorothy Parker. *She deigned to live in Hollywood*, the flyleaf read.

Once a year, at Easter, I would meet Wally for a vacation. He paid, I chose. Paris, London, Rome, Vienna.

"What's wrong with L.A.? That you might love it?" Wally said every year.

Wally loved L.A. He loved the freeways. The Hollywood sign. Grauman's Chinese. Rodeo Drive. Nothing was too vulgar to capture his affections. His girlfriends, a series of them, were uniformly tall, blond and vapid.

"They've got nothing in their heads," I complained.

"Of course not. They're above the tree line," Wally reported.

"You're a cliché," I warned.

"And you?" Wally countered.

We were on dangerous ground. How do you tell someone your life is a standard, an example, a choice over lesser choices, not merely the end product of conditioning? You can't. That's why I caved in about the Hamptons. Also, I loved my brother.

And so, at four-thirty on a steamy Friday afternoon, I was chugging, lurching and sweltering toward the Hamptons. About Far Rockaway, I noticed Peter's stories slapping at my consciousness, a regular, repetitive *slap-slap-slap* like the tiny wavelets off Long Island Sound.

She had the face of a funerary urn... he described an embittered dowager.

His brow was swept clean as a deck, he described his thoughtless hero.

My brow, meanwhile, was furrowed by annoyance. The Pakistani behind me smelled heavily of patchouli, a smell I associated with Wally's defection to the West Coast. I caught a glimpse of myself in the window as an inbound train swept by us. My face resembled a funerary urn. What were the ashes? My youth?

At forty-one, I was still a vibrant woman—if I could ever be said to be a vibrant woman. My figure was trim. My stride sturdy, if not buoyant. Even to my own ear, this inner inventory smacked alarmingly of Miss Marple. A fondness for mysteries is my secret passion. I indulge it as harmless, bingeing on weekends away from the Magazine, gobbling detective stories the way our secretary, Kaye, sneaks Fannie May, Ghirardelli, Lindt, Godiva.

Do I need to explain that for an editor of my standing, a taste for mysteries is guilty pleasure? Foggy nights, trench coats, the varying calibers and attributes of Berettas, pistols and classic Colts; scarlet lips, low-slung roadsters, the shattered urn on the library floor—

I was the shattered urn, I thought suddenly, but we were pulling into the station. Wally stood waving to me from the platform. Bronzed, casual, he looked like my younger brother, my son. When had I become the spinster he had seen me for? Emily, for Dickinson: a rose by any other name, but a spinster by this one?

"Wally!" Wally smelled of lime and something mustier. "Not patchouli, after all these years?"

"Gianfranco Ferre," Wally corrected me. "It has a low, woody subnote. Vertiver. Just read the ads."

"Mmphh."

"Em, Em, this is Peter."

For the first time, I noticed the man standing a discreet distance away from us. Like Wally, he was bronzed, fit, an Armani Adonis.

"How do you do?"

"The legendary Emily."

I looked closer. Was he mocking me? His eyes were chocolate brown and guileless. His smile was quick, white and open. The hand that shook mine was tensile with an easy strength. A tennis player, I speculated. Such speculations were a hobby of mine; amateur sleuthing, perhaps, born from my secret vice. Good for my work, though, I told myself routinely. An editor must be specific. The faint line on his third finger left hand, the hand grasping my Hermès travel bag: a divorcé—a recent one, evidently. Oh, no, not again, Wally?

"You look alarmed," Peter said.

"Exhausted, annoyed, hungry," I countered.

"Emily is very specific," Wally volunteered.

They were driving a Range Rover, the first one I ever saw, olive drab, one of those muddy, muted "earth tones," like their expensive linen shirts.

"What are those funny things in the front?" I asked.

"Rhino bars," Wally answered.

"*Rhino* bars?"

"Custom bumper," Peter explained. He cut me a glance. I could see he was sizing me up, measuring me against Wally's description.

"Cut it out," I told him.

"What?" Good, he was startled.

"Stop. Staring. It's vulgar. Back East."

"Ah, yes, back East," Wally interceded.

"He was looking at me like a potted plant," I snapped. Let's get any nonsense about a romance over with.

"Like a wallflower," Peter put in suddenly. "A faded damask rose in a Victorian sitting room."

"Charming description." I glared bullets at Wally. He shrugged, guiltless as ever. Movie people. My brother had become one, and they had no shame.

The plan was a simple country weekend. As if the Hamptons were either simple or country. Before we left the parking lot, I spotted three people I knew.

"Get me out of here," I growled as people waved gaily.

"She's a recluse," Wally explained.

"Arugula?" Peter asked.

"I'm sorry?"

"Do you like it?"

"Yes. I suppose so."

"Peter has decided to retire and become an arugula farmer."

"Retire from what?"

"Actually? I'm a writer."

"Really?" I brightened. "We might have something in common after all."

"Oh, I doubt that," Wally put in. "Peter writes movies."

"You mean you're a *screenwriter*?"

"Disdain colors her words like a faint Japanese wash, doesn't it, Wally?" Peter asked.

"I'm staying out of this."

"Think of me as an arugula farmer if it's any easier," Peter counseled me.

I'm sure you remember the storm, or read about it, at least. By ten P.M. Friday we were socked in with small craft warnings. By eleven, a gale warning was in effect. The news at midnight called it a hurricane. The electricity went out moments later and I found myself, for the first time in years, unable to read myself to sleep.

At dinner, Peter had been pleasant enough company—charming, really. And his arugula salad was delicious. He seemed to find me amusing, for reasons of his own, I guessed. I was not my best and brightest. Why should I be? He was a stranger intruding on my reunion weekend with Wally.

"Disdain colors her words like a faint Japanese wash." For some reason, Peter's comment snagged in my thoughts. Trying to sleep, unable to read, I played this sentence over and over. It was somehow so literary. And what was that description of me? "A faded damask rose in a Victorian sitting room." That was unnerving too. Who was this man—or who did he think he was—that he could make such dismissive remarks?

He's glib, facile, a *movie* person, I reminded myself.

"Nonsense, I'm an arugula farmer," I could hear him chuckling from the adjacent room. I slept fitfully.

By morning, the shutter on my dormer window had torn loose. I woke to a sheet of water pouring down the windowpane and in over the sill. The Victorian washstand near the window sported a small embroidered towel. I grabbed the pretty frippery and swabbed at the floor.

"You really need a rag," Peter observed, appearing in the bedroom doorway.

"Can't you knock?" I asked. "Or don't they do that in California?"

"Scorn withered her prose like late-autumn weeds.... The door was standing open."

"Stop being so literary. Get me a rag. This is a flood."

"An official nor'easter. There's no stopping the elements. Pretty nightdress."

"Do you *mind*?"

Wally, not Peter, returned with a rag. We'd rented the house furnished—and expensively. The little embroidered hand towel was clearly ruined, running all directions in three different colors from its gaily dyed embroidered yarns. The shutter was torn off.

The puddle on the fine hardwood floor was making havoc with the wax job. I felt a frowsy mess myself, wild and disheveled; not my city self, not by a mile.

"What's that noise?"

It was a tiny, whiny bell.

"That's breakfast," Wally replied.

"What does he think we're doing? *Howards End*?" I demanded.

"No, I imagine *Upstairs, Downstairs*," Wally answered.

So, I was a snob. If he wished, I'd concede him that. What was snobbery but standards in action? I descended the stairs one step at a time. Something smelled heavenly. Peter was working some thinly sliced potatoes in a heavy wrought-iron skillet.

"*Pommes frites?*"

"Hash browns," Peter told me. "*Pommes frites* to you."

I was dismayed to see that in broad daylight Wally's friend Peter looked even more attractive than he had the night before.

"You're staring," he said.

"Intellectual curiosity," I offered.

"Nonsense. Lust."

"I beg your pardon?"

"No need. You can lust after me anytime."

"Wally?" I appealed to my brother, who sipped his orange juice and stared at the rain.

"Mmm?"

"He's insufferable!"

"Takes one to know one."

"I did not come out here to be insulted."

"Neither did I," Peter said. "I may be a humble arugula farmer, but I still feel disappointments keenly. I know when I've been spurned."

"Sarcasm," I replied. "From the Greek. To eat or tear flesh."

"I told you she was like this," Wally intoned, cutting a sideways glance.

"I like her. She has a face like a funerary urn," Peter responded softly. He was dishing pommes frites, a pesto omelette, a side of garden tomatoes.

"*You*," I said evenly.

"They were good stories," he said defiantly. "Orange juice? Coffee?"

"How dare you!"

"Oh, God, she's cute when she's mad, Wally."

Wally looked from one to the other like we were staging a personal Wimbledon. Perhaps we were. East meets West. An editor meets her comeuppance. A writer meets his Waterloo.

"I miss something?" Wally inquired absently.

"Your sister rejected my stories," Peter said stubbornly. His jaw pushed out like a little boy's.

"Oh, for God's sake. They were about the movies," I snapped. I started my eggs.

"What does that mean?" Peter and Wally asked simultaneously. Lightning cracked not a hundred feet away.

"One, two, three..." I counted, waiting for thunder. It came on "four" with a deafening boom.

"Near miss," Wally said.

"No. She called them *bright little things*."

"What?" Wally was lost.

"His stories," I replied.

"Were they?"

"Bright little things?"

"I told you. They were about the movies."

"What does that mean?" Peter and Wally asked again, together.

"I hate the movies."

"So what?" Wally pressed. "How were the stories?"

"They were about the movies," I repeated.

"Write about what you know," Peter said quietly, earnestly. I looked up from my eggs. He sat across the table from me, staring right through me.

"Write about what you know," he repeated.

For an alarming moment, I thought his eyes were wet with tears. Writers! Why do they have to be so sensitive?

"Writers! Why do you have to be so sensitive?" I exploded.

"So we can write!" Peter exploded back. For a moment, I thought he was going to hurl his Portmeirion Botanic Garden plate straight to the floor.

"Stop it, you two!" Now Wally exploded. "This is ridiculous, over a couple of stupid little stories."

"They were wonderful stories," I shot back. "And you stay out of this."

"Wait a minute." Peter grabbed my hand across the table. "They were?"

"Were what?"

"Wonderful stories."

"Of course. I just hate movies."

"Why?"

"Oh, who knows? Who cares? I hate movie people, I suppose."

Wally choked on his pommes frites, but Peter burst out laughing. He laughed so hard tears ran down the sides of his cheeks. He hiccuped and coughed, gasped for breath.

"What's so funny?" I demanded.

Wally studied his eggs. "I'm a movie people," he protested. "Ingenuous, grandiose, childlike, given to wild enthusiasm."

"Wally, you're her brother," Peter interjected. "I'm sure that's different."

I don't like change. I don't care if it's for the better, as they say. I liked my bookish summers holed up in the city. I liked my non-movie people at the Magazine. I liked myself, for that matter. I couldn't really be the priggish, bigoted, callow person I abruptly saw mirrored to me that weekend. Could I?

Wally called, asking me back out.

"Will *he* be there?"

"Peter?"

"Yes, Peter. Don't act so innocent. What a monster."

"I knew you two liked each other."

Liked? How could I like a man who showed me to be such a fool? No, when I stormed out of the house that weekend, plunging through the streets of pouring rain—hiking to where?—not even the trains were running. I did not feel affection! Drenched to the skin, sulking in the Range Rover, I felt—

"I hate him, Wally. Keep it up and I'll hate you too."

"He thought you were super."

"Don't lie to me."

"Why would I lie to you?"

The truth was, Wally never had lied to me, favoring, even as a youngster, the aggression of the unvarnished truth. And so, when the two dozen red roses arrived at the Magazine, accompanied by a note reading only *Forgive me*, I suspected they might be from Peter. And when my air-conditioning conked out, I phoned Wally and said I'd be on the one-forty.

My train was met by Peter, wearing a subdued mud brown shirt that matched the interior of the Range Rover, which also looked subdued. It looked denuded, like a man minus his accustomed mustache. It took me a minute to register that the rhino bars were missing.

"You shaved," I said.

Peter grabbed my travel bag and shrugged.

"Mustaches are for the West."

Great, I thought. Not only a Californian, but a psychic. A crazy. A loon—no, loons were indigenous to the East, weren't they?

Although, hadn't I seen them on Lake Tahoe? "I think they have them in Tahoe." My God, I was talking out loud! "Excuse me!" I said. "I'm so sorry."

"Me too. You got the roses."

"Mmm-hmm. *At the Magazine.*"

"Was that a mistake?"

"An intrusion."

"Ah. Sorry again."

Peter opened my car door, handed me up. Chivalry wasn't dead. It just lived in someplace called the Malibu Colony. No wonder I didn't experience it very often.

"They were lovely."

"Bright little things," Peter jabbed.

"I meant the roses."

"So did I."

If chivalry wasn't dead, it was going to be. This man inspired murder in my heart.

"Penny for your thoughts."

"They were a cliché."

"Ouch!" Peter accelerated alarmingly.

"A big, corny, beautiful cliché. We're all used to the stray branch of lilac dragged in from the country garden."

"Oh, back to the roses! We're used to Technicolor roses, blooms the size of small nuclear explosions. Two dozen seemed a modest amount."

"Thanks for the discretion, in that case."

"Anytime. It's my middle name."

Discretion was Peter's middle name, just not in any recognizable form. One weekend in July, he rented an entire movie theater.

"We're having a screening party," he told me at the train station. I handed him my bag. "Maybe I'll stay home and read."

I would have too, but neither Peter nor Wally would divulge what they were screening. Prompted by curiosity, I abandoned my virtuous plan, leaving my manuscripts in a messy stack on my bed. The screening was at seven, and I was sneaking a quick glance at an old Ellery Queen when the scent of popcorn came wafting up the stairs. Popcorn! This was too corny.

"Is that a joke?" Peter asked when I voiced this opinion.

"Of course it's a joke," Wally answered for me. "As well as one of Em's most deeply held convictions. A cliché? Off with your head! She's an editor."

"Wait a minute," I protested. "Some clichés are acceptable. But we call those classics."

"Like a 1963 Chevy truck," Wally put in.

"The Righteous Brothers and popcorn," Peter added.

The popcorn may have been a cliché, but it was delicious. We lugged it to the theater in great greasy bags.

"Where *is* everybody?" I asked when seven P.M. came and went.

"We are everybody," Peter answered. "Didn't you always suspect we movie people thought that?"

"Mmm." I felt immediately guilty, but blamed it on the popcorn. Real butter. Gobs of it.

"What are we seeing?" I pestered.

"Ssh!" sshed Peter.

On screen, a wind came up and a sandstorm swirled, revealing and concealing some vintage planes.

"Is this an old movie?" I whispered.

"A good one," Wally said in a tone that added, "Please shut up."

I shut up. For the next nearly three hours I sat silent and enthralled. I broke silence only once, to burst out, "Where did you get those stars?!" thinking, Canada? Some clean air belt somewhere.

"Special effects," Peter whispered just as the screen filled with billowing, roiling clouds that could be nothing but special effects.

The movie, in case you haven't guessed, was something called

Close Encounters of the Third Kind. By Steven Spielberg. I had no idea he was so talented.

"I'm sure he says the same of you," Wally tweaked me.

As his tan faded, he became more bookish and less glorious, Peter almost fit in the Hamptons. At the least, he did a credible job of passing. To my surprise, after the initial shock of change wore off, I enjoyed what became my regular weekends. I enjoyed the literary parties where Peter was often my escort and I, not a wallflower, but the belle of the ball.

I would arrive on Fridays, laden with well-intentioned manuscripts and a secret cache of mysteries. I would ignore both in favor of long beach rambles, alone or in Peter's company. He and Wally were collaborating on a script for a major director whom they infuriatingly left nameless. Not that I cared about movie people, per se, but the mystery, the intrigue they drew about the project spoke—and loudly—to my secret vice.

Calling it mystery loves company, I began spending more and more time with Peter, plying him for details. If not plot, then character. If not character, then genre.

"Romance," Peter finally anted up, the same day our beach perambulations yielded me a rare crenelated shell. It was hard to say which discovery pleased me more.

"A romance!"

I couldn't picture Wally writing a romance. And Peter? I began to believe he could write anything he turned his hand to. I based this on my thorough (uninvited) scrutiny of the scripts and manuscripts he left strewn around the house. I didn't snoop, exactly—oh, yes, I did.

Peter (discretion was his middle name) had not told me he wrote mysteries. *Perry Mason, Murder, She Wrote*—murder, he wrote, and I read whatever I could lay my hands on. His stories, the ones he'd sent to the Magazine, were wonderful. His mysteries, even in screenplay form, were better, positively addicting. Why, I wondered, had he ever bent his imagination into a topiary niceness (or his version of it) merely to publish in the Magazine? This was another mystery.

The last weekend in August, on a night cooler than the others, with bright stars, Peter and I drove home very late from a particularly raucous literary party. I had drunk too much wine, a white, icy Corvo. The bright, diamond-hard points of starlight seemed blurred and enlarged like the stars on a muzzy greeting card or the larger-than-life, extra-twinkly, induced stars created by special effects in the movies.

"How's your romance going?" I asked. "The one you're collaborating on with Wally?"

"Very well, I think....Did I say I was collaborating with Wally?"

Had he?...Hadn't he?

"I thought so—and the two of you were so conspiratorial."

"We were, weren't we?"

Peter drove with a relaxed and easy hand. He looked pleased with himself. Even from the corner of my eye I could see that much. I decided to stir things up a little bit.

"So, who were you collaborating with, then?"

Peter cut me a quick glance.

"Why, you, of course," he said.

Our house in the Malibu Colony is two doors from Wally's. It looks like a shoe box tipped on its ear. "It's awful," my friends from the East often blurt out, some defiant, some inadvertent.

"Of course it is," I agree. "You know how movie people are. There's no accounting for their taste."

SALT

Casting Call

[WIFEY] Star-crossed and double-crossed, our narrator is strong in the broken places—an actress with enough character to write a happy ending.... LEAD (216) POSSIBLE NUDITY.

SALT

The he first time I met Patricia was in a New York City hotel room—mine. She came in trailing clouds of glory—or at least two of the country's most eligible husbands. One of them was mine. The other was hers, recently estranged. She sent hers off to bed, "Because you've got to catch that early flight." Looking a little relieved, he did just what she asked. That left the three of us.

Patricia was producing my husband Michael's film, an updated, reenvisioned *Frankenstein*. I was only starring in it, playing the bride. I was, in fact, my husband's bride. We were veterans of a decade's living together and a new belated marriage—in honor of our upcoming child ("Henry" if a boy; "Hannah" if a girl). Michael was a hot director and I was a hot young star myself. We got married to layouts in *Vogue*, that kind of PR presence. We both found this a hoot.

When I met Michael, I was waitressing at Max's Kansas City and he was finishing a master's at NYU. The master's was in film, of course, and its primary advantage, he said, was that it gave him access to equipment. He had no intention of being "an academic."

I knew what he meant. I'd grown up in Hollywood and that was how I felt about the movies. At five-foot-ten, I'd been hit on by would-be agents since I was thirteen. No, I wanted a life away from all that. With that in mind I used my graduation money for a one-way ticket to New York. I was studying at the Neighborhood Playhouse and planning a life on the stage. Michael changed that faster than you could say fast forward. Do you remember that backlit shot of Giancarlo Giannini at the top of the stairs in Lina Wertmüller's—never mind. But that's how good Michael looked looming in the doorway, only taller and American. He was a regular. One night at the end of my shift, he came in for a drink and asked me to star in the underground film he was making. I said yes because I wanted to date him.

Predictably, my theater friends considered this a massive defection. I was slumming, they said, and they were right. Michael's "underground" film involved vampires on the subways. Although I would end up the Vampire Queen, I began as a victim—of course I was: a victim of love. Within a month, I was living with him.

"Good Michael" I called Michael, sometimes to his face. (My last boyfriend had been "Bad Brad," a rock-and-roll drummer with a heroin habit.) Good Michael with his wild energy and enthusiasm—he loved *all* movies and almost everything else, for that matter—made me feel rescued, not only from Bad Brad, but from the backbiting and competition that seemed as much a part of theater as the curtains.

Good Michael liked to go to Chinatown at three A.M. If I demurred, he would bring home egg rolls and feed them to me between kisses at dawn. Not that all of it was about sex, but Good Michael practiced tantric love, scrubbed my back, rubbed my feet, and taught me how to walk on his very long spine to get the kinks out of it. He taught me to eat sushi. I began to feel like a geisha and love the role.

For that matter, I loved any role he gave me. Vampire Queen of the subway. Born-again mummy of the Metropolitan. Michael's films became known for their kinky wit and I became a star of the underground, a diva of downtown. I say "diva" because Michael convinced me I could sing. Our last "little" movie, the one that was our breakthrough with the critics, cast me as a torch-singing zombie—a look I shared with Grace Jones.

Patricia's movie, Michael's "new, bigger, real-budget *Frankenstein*," was our shot at the big time.

I haven't said yet that the buzz on our picture was already active and very good. Word had it that this picture would make stars of all concerned. I took this to be Patricia's doing. She was always showing up on set in leather micro-minis, cleavage and a bomber jacket, a journalist on one arm. I'd seen her throw one long thigh around the leg of a startled *New York Times* reporter. To his surprise, not mine, he wrote we movie folks were wonderful.

Speaking of which...

"Pour me a drink," Patricia said, collapsing on my bed. "Oh, by the way. I'm thirsty."

As if I didn't know.

Patricia was thirty years old, hooked on cocaine and fond of Stolichnaya. My husband thought she was brilliant. Of course he did. She loved his project. She thought he was a genius. Aside from my obvious function, I don't think she thought about me at all.

Patricia coproduced with her estranged husband. He did pre- and postproduction. She liked the combat zone of line producing. They'd just swapped coasts and now we had her full-time.

Ours was an A-list movie. Patricia wore straight A clothes, Armani and Alaïa. She had legs to forever and balls up there some-where—if you believed the stories. Personally, I believed them.

"Where's that drink?" Patricia sniffed the air like a Doberman.

"Call Room Service."

"Oooh, Michael, she's a wittew bit angwee."

"I'm pregnant. It's two A.M. I have to look good in the morn-ing. You know that. You're the producer. Go home."

Pregnancy made me a straight-shooter.

"She's off her feed," Michael volunteered.

I certainly was. Morning sickness hit most afternoons at three. Hormones gave my skin a rosy glow. The camera loved me but I sometimes had to vomit between takes. Our costume designer, the bona fide genius if you asked me, said she could cover me for about six more weeks—with luck, that would be enough.

Patricia spoke up.

"You're right. You're right. You're right. The pressure's getting to me. I have to go home to bed—my lonely bed. Myself. It's just that Michael's such good company."

"Ditto," Michael returned. "We'll do it again."

("It" being drinks and brainstorming each night after we wrapped.)

Now I spoke up.

"Great, you two, but why not wait until we get the film in the can?"

"Uh-oh. Wifey's really mad at me....Good night, Wifey," Patricia cooed, crawling across the bed on her hands and feet, rump in the air. "Sweet dreams, Wifey." I dove under the pillow.

Michael showed her to the door.

"She's a bitch, Michael," I said when the door closed behind her miles of legs.

"Just high-strung," he assured me. "A couple of drinks keep the doctor away. She sees that celebrity shrink team? What's their name?"

"Desi and Lucy. I don't know. Could we go to sleep?"

Jesus. Did he think we were made of iron? Pregnancy had made me newly aware of my own physical limits.

The next day on set, Patricia presented me with a dozen blood-red roses. In a bold, slanting hand, the crisp little florist's card read *Dear Mommy, please forgive your bad girl. I admire you so. Patricia.*

"You do look beautiful, you know," she told me between setups. "No one would guess you were incubating a little genius."

"I'll try to bear it in mind," I told her. My irony went undetected.

Returning to my trailer for lunch, I found a Christian Dior baptismal gown draped on the back of my makeup chair.

It was lovely. I was furious.

"What's eating you?" Michael wanted to know.

"Oh, saltines and green apples. The pectin's good for nausea. What do you mean, what's 'eating' me? Maybe I want to pick my own baptismal gown."

"I thought it was very generous."

"Pushy."

"C'mon. She means well. She's just a kid, remember?"

"Since when did I graduate to the geriatric set?"

"She's thirty."

"Big deal. I'm thirty-five and look how immature I can be." Michael gave me a look that told me he was thinking that and worse. I felt a flip in my stomach that did not feel like baby. "Tell her it's lovely, Michael."

At thirty-five, I might not have been older and wiser, but I did know when to fold my cards. Clearly, any criticism of Patricia was not in my own best interests. All right, I was an actress. I would act friendly. That night at dailies, when Michael and Patricia planned their nightly drink, I asked to join them. We could all be friends.

"It's really a kind of director-producer thing," Michael told me.

"Don't be so mean, Mikey," Patricia interceded on my behalf. "Besides, I haven't talked any decent female nonsense in forever."

"It's private," Michael insisted. "Creative colleagues."

"Another time," I said. My stomach was flipping again.

"Oh, bosh. He just doesn't want you to know about my blow. I do the occasional line of coke. To relax." Patricia kissed my cheek. "We'll be home early, Mom. Don't worry."

I began to see how I had suddenly become the geriatric set.

We wrapped the movie midway through my second trimester. Patricia, for reasons known only to herself, planned to hold the wrap party at a Hell's Kitchen sex club. She sent Michael a gold-plated dildo and a note that read *You did it, you fuck* in her bold, slanting hand. I again got blood-red roses, slightly wilted.

"And she likes us!" I joked to Michael.

"She's just trying to be witty," Michael defended her. "Sometimes you're a real ice cube," he added. "Patricia says she's intimidated by you."

By then I was used to the ongoing saga of poor Patricia, how unequipped she was to "swim with the sharks," as she put it. How clever, I thought, for Patricia to position herself as the underdog with Michael. Good Michael was notoriously kindhearted. This impulse in him ran deeper than liberal guilt. It was a guiding principle, his "fairness rule," as I called it. Patricia had managed to persuade him that she was needier of his attentions than I, his pregnant wife. She should have been the actress, I thought bitterly.

Naively, I imagined Patricia and Michael's bond to be self-limiting. Patricia's husband was supposed to take over for postproduction. All I had to do was get through the actual shoot and then...The plan was two weeks in Tahiti and then into the cutting room. Just hold on until Tahiti, I told myself. I imagined Michael and myself intricately intertwined in a hemp hammock slung between two obliging palms. Call it too many Club Med ads or the sporadic cessation of my nausea, call it daydreaming or denial, I really thought our sojourn would be sheer romance, the filmmaker's version of the Kama Sutra, love under—and amid—the stars. Just hold on until we wrap, I told myself.

My sister Linda, long-distance from L.A., told me the same thing. Linda, a gun-toting member of the L.A.P.D. vice squad, was not fond of Michael and his liberal ways. Nonetheless, she tried to help me with her version of sisterly advice.

"Look. You know I've never liked the guy, but you love him, so stick it out. Besides, you're knocked up."

"Maybe I'm just being paranoid."

"No, you're definitely knocked up."

"Very funny. I meant about her. She did send me roses."

"A rose by any other name is a bitch," Linda said. "And I thought she was dating what's-his-name. The one with the extraterrestrials."

"No. She's dating the one with the gizmos. She's producing the one with the extraterrestrials. That's all."

"Well, pretend that's all she's doing with Michael and when you get back from Paradise, we'll spend your remaining pregnancy at the movies. We'll go see *Bringing Up Baby*."

"That baby was a cheetah."

"Michael's a cheater. We'll make it work."

"Linda, I don't absolutely know that Michael's cheating on me. Maybe I'm just paranoid."

"Ever see *Gaslight*? She was right, he was trying to kill her."

"Michael is not trying to kill me."

"Matter of opinion."

"Linda, you have the mind of a vice cop."

If you've seen one sex club—which admittedly, you may not have—you've seen them all. They're dark and feature performers in cages and enough leather to start a boot factory. The boot was what I hoped to give Patricia. We were seated in a ringside booth enjoying simulated (?) intercourse and what passed for conversation. Patricia, of course, was the one talking.

"I envy you so. Flying off to Tahiti. Alone together, just the three of you." She reached across the booth and patted my stomach. "When do you have to quit having sex?"

"When you *die*," I told her.

"I have nobody," she continued. "That's why Mikey has been so kind to me. Taking pity on an old maid."

Old maid? This was a new wrinkle—and the only one she had.

"Come with," Michael offered. "Tahiti would do you good."

"Really?"

"Really. Okay by you, honey?"

(I was too stunned to answer.)

"Thank you, Daddy. Thank you, Mommy." (So much for the old-maid routine.) Patricia abruptly burst into tears, or at least sniffles, but whether it was from her emotions or her coke habit was hard to tell. "This cold makes me so emotional," she added.

"Ah, Michael?" One of the overhead swinging cages was veering wildly in our direction, propelled by the exertions of its occupants. I was in danger of being fucked upon, not just fucked over.

"Oh, dear, Mikey. Wifey looks queasy."

"No. But I'm a little tired and I don't want to catch your cold."

I said this sweetly and gestured to Patricia's dripping nose.

"Yeah. It's hung on forever, hasn't it?" Patricia's newest fashion accessory was a penchant for impeccably milled men's handkerchiefs.

Michael sneezed. Patricia patted his arm in sympathy.

"Careful. You know how you genius directors always get sick when you wrap."

"I may have caught it already." Michael leaned over and gave me a brotherly, dismissive kiss on the cheek. "Good night, honey. The driver can take you to the hotel."

The driver did take me back to the hotel, where I promptly called Linda. It was midnight, but only nine in L.A.

"I thought tonight was the wrap party," she said.

"I got pooped. I came home."

"You came home alone? Where's Michael?"

"Oh, downtown at this sex club with Patricia."

"What?"

"They're holding the wrap party there."

"I'm surprised they didn't hire hookers."

"Actually? So am I. Patricia and Michael keep talking in the press about Frankenstein as an 'erotic monster.' Someone should explain to them that not *all* power is sexy."

"Glad to see you can still think straight. Unlike your buddies, as I understand."

Linda waited for me to take the bait....I did.

"What have you heard?"

"There's a lot of talk about it turning into a coke movie. Your husband—"

"My husband is a wonderful filmmaker. He has great taste in neckties, is a fine sushi chef, sings beautifully in the shower, drives a car like Mario Andretti, doesn't get my jokes but has beautiful shoulders."

"I'll tell it to the judge."

"C'mon, Linda. Coke's not addictive."

"Who told you that? Enjoy Bali H'ai. Call if you need me. We could always go to Club Med instead."

"Thanks."

Tahiti with Patricia *was* like Club Med—constant noise, constant sexual tension—between her and Michael, unfortunately. While director and producer enjoyed sun and surf, I enjoyed the return of waves of nausea and paranoia. I was having ominous cramps that seemed to surface whenever they disappeared together. I knew that Michael's travel bags contained Quaaludes, which were wonderful for cramps, among other things, but I was off all drugs for the duration of my pregnancy. That meant no Quaaludes—not to mention no alcohol, cigarettes or caffeine.

Michael and Patricia made up for my temperance.

"Too bad you can't celebrate with us," Patricia consoled me. "It must be so boring. I promise you a magnum of champagne in the recovery room."

Patricia delivered this promise early one morning as she and Michael were icing up their supplies for the day at the beach. The day before, there had been reports of a great white shark spotted offshore.

I wasn't about to swim pregnant in shark-infested waters. I wasn't crazy about Michael doing it either.

"Don't you two worry?" I asked.

"I love to swim with sharks. That's why I'm swimming with Michael," Patricia purred.

"This thing was sixteen feet long," I badgered.

"We're fine. Get some sleep." Michael kissed my brow like I was his aging mother.

As it happened, I did sleep as they swam amid the sharks. I slept and I dreamed. I fell asleep to the drone of the ceiling fan and the rush and ebb of the surf breaking first at the reef and then, more gently, at the shore. Sleeping, I dreamed of a great, dark snake, a viper, coiled in the corner of Michael's and my bedroom.

I woke panting and drenched with sweat. I couldn't wait to get back to the real viper's nest, L.A.

"Bali H'ai calling and now the Steenbeck," Michael caroled gaily, off to edit the first day back home. He pecked me on the cheek. "Off to the editing room, where destiny beckons. Oh! If Patricia calls, tell her to bring Rock and meet me there."

"Rock?"

"She'll know."

By then, so did I.

Of course, Patricia was the viper. Instead of an apple, she offered Michael power—the traditional offering. More accurately, she offered him feelings of power. She carried them with her in a big white rock. She kept the rock in a little leather pouch—except when she was chipping at it. She and Michael chipped at it a lot.

I told myself, just carry the baby safely to term. That's your only job. Michael will be back. One day, you will wake up and your husband, Good Michael, will be home and all of this will be just an ugly dream. Besides, coke wasn't really addicting....

"It's addictive," Linda said. "It's a class-A drug. It's a class-A drug because it's addictive. They're coke whores," she advised me. "Let me bust them."

"He's the father of my child."

"Don't remind me."

Addictive or not, it was clearly mind-altering.

Michael stayed in the cutting room for longer and longer stretches, arriving home edgy and unable to sleep. My own sleep was restless from the swimming motions of the child within me. Many nights, I felt like the baby was doing laps—while Michael was doing sit-ups.

"What was that?" He would lurch awake, shooting bolt upright. "I want you to get a gun."

"I don't want a gun, Michael. Go back to sleep."

"Didn't you hear it? There's somebody outside. You stay here. I'll have a look around."

Night after night, Michael patrolled our property. Never mind the Bel-Air police hovering low in their copters. They were not protection, just confirmation, to Michael.

"Someone's out there. There's something they're not telling us."

"Maybe it's just your nerves."

"Maybe it's not. I'm getting a gun."

Michael got a gun.

Where was the Good Michael? I wondered. Did that Michael still exist? This Michael barked orders whenever he was crossed, punched a hole through the bedroom wall, punched another through the stereo speaker.

"Can't you hear the static?" this Michael roared.

"Yes, but I thought it was between us."

"Very funny. I'm getting a dog."

"What kind of dog? The baby's coming."

"Maybe a Rottweiler."

Michael got the dog. Brutus. A Rottweiler. To my relief and Michael's disappointment, a kinder soul was never born. When Michael began sleeping at the cutting room, Brutus commandeered his side of the bed. One night, when the alarm shrilled unexpectedly, Brutus successfully cornered a very frightened kitten, which had come in through an open window. The kitten was black—and bad luck, Michael said. I kept it anyway. It was homeless.

"Just don't expect me to change the kitty litter—and don't you change it, either. You'll get whatchamacallit. The thing you get from changing cat shit when you're pregnant."

"I don't use kitty litter. I leave the window to the garden open."

"Great. Cat shit in the garden. My favorite."

"She's an orphan, Michael. I call her Annie."

Brutus grew quite fond of Annie. Michael was not impressed. Nothing warm or friendly or loving seemed to touch him anymore. Increasingly, his talk was of power, violence and revenge. I knew about Michael's gun—guns—but I never saw or heard one until the night he shot out the hallway mirror, having sighted his image as an intruder.

"I can't live like this" I told him, after the police were gone.

"Is that an ultimatum?"

"I think it's just a fact."

"Well, neither can I. I'm moving a cot into the cutting room."

And he did.

Michael and Patricia were cutting off the lot in an editing room on La Brea. I stopped by one night on the way to a movie with my sister. I left my sister in the car and climbed the metal staircase that led to the second floor suite. The door to the suite was locked.

"Knock-knock."

"Who's there?" (Michael.)

"Me."

"Me who?" (Michael.)

"Michael, open the door." (Unmistakably Patricia.)

Michael opened the door. I hadn't seen him for days and neither had the sandman. He and Patricia sported darkly circled eyes and a snowy pallor. Both were dressed in matching chinos and T-shirts. The windows had blackout shades. The "cot" was a black leather couch with a matching black lacquer coffee table. The table had white racing stripes, a dozen of them, running its full length.

"It's you." Michael patted my stomach and avoided my eyes.

"Is it you? You look pooped, sweetheart."

"He looks divine. He's a genius. You should see what he's doing with this film."

"You look pretty pooped too, Patricia."

"Do I? How decadent. What price art! I hope to accept my award looking like Nosferatu."

"You've got a good shot at it—there's a resemblance. I don't know about the award."

"Hey, c'mon, you two. No catfights."

I rose above Michael's characterization. "I just wanted you to know that Linda and I were going to be at the movies. In case you called home and I didn't answer."

"Where's Linda?" Linda had always made Michael nervous.

"Is she the sister?" Evidently, she made Patricia nervous too.

"Yes. *The one I told you about.*" Michael was speaking in italics.

"She's out in the car," I said.

"No, I'm not," Linda said from just behind me. "I'm right here." With that, she stepped into the room and grabbed my elbow. "C'mon. You don't need this. We're going to be late.

Jesus Christ! What's all that?"

Patricia stepped forward. "My name is Patricia."

"That." Linda pointed to the racing stripes of coke squiggled the length of the table. (I had told her about "Rock.")

"*That?*" Michael laughed nervously. "That's salt."

"Right! Right!" Patricia co-signed. "If you've got movies, you've got to have popcorn and if you have popcorn, you've got to have salt!"

"So, where's the popcorn?"

"We ate it."

"Right." My sister stepped forward and shoved Michael in the chest. "Fuck you, Michael. She's having your baby."

"Linda, please, let's get out of here."

"I ought to bust you two. Maybe I will—"

"Linda!" Now I was grabbing her by the arm. "Please, Linda, let's just leave."

"Good idea," Michael said.

"Let me talk to her, Michael." Patricia put an arm out and laid a hand on my sister's shoulder. It was the same kind of move I'd seen her use to cozy up to the press. "We did eat it, but we didn't use the salt because, you see, I'm premenstrual and retaining water and—"

"Fuck you too." (*The New York Times* might have bought Patricia's stories, but not my kid sister.)

"Maybe we should go now," I volunteered again.

"Great!" Michael gave me a peck and Linda a hug that shoved us out the door. Linda was fuming.

"What a jerk. Be careful on the stairs. What an asshole."

"I love him."

"You're pathetic."

I was dizzy and clutched for the railing. What is it about going sane that feels just like going crazy?

"He's not coming back, is he?"

"I don't think so."

For the baby's sake, not Michael's, I saw no evil, heard no evil, spoke no evil—not even when *The National Enquirer* showed up on my doorstep with tales of Michael and Patricia's rendezvous in the hospital parking lot the night that our daughter, Hannah, was born.

"You should tell the whole world what a rat he is," Linda urged predictably.

"Why? So our daughter could grow up and read about it?"

In short, I was impeccable. I was also numb.

When our film received unexpectedly bad reviews, Patricia dumped Michael for a certain very famous ballet star. In a flurry of tabloid press, Michael left for Japan and points east with his best friend, a rock star. Reports of their sightings were published regularly in *Rolling Stone*. I knew he had a nosebleed in Hiroshima and sang in a karioke club in Tokyo. I took these reports to mean that Bad Michael was still in evidence and so was "salt."

Michael traveled to New Delhi and from there to Tibet. His tabloid trail grew colder. Who would return? I wondered. Which Michael? Hannah learned to walk. She did not learn to say "Dada," although she was very precocious in every other way.

Michael stayed out of the country nearly a year. When he came home, his business manager revealed a million-dollar debt to him and Michael left Hollywood in disgust, moving to San Francisco. Good Michael? Bad Michael? No Michael returned to me.

Michael's avoidance of me "was a sign of undealt-with feelings," my therapist assured me. And a sign of the times? I wondered. I would see Michael's picture in the paper, especially after he cleaned up and his career became what it was meant to be, and I would think, You are the father of my child. The man I lived with and loved for ten years. Who are you, that you could walk away? Michael never answered me.

"It was the 'salt,'" my sister would assure me. "He associates you with that."

Maybe people are disposable and I just couldn't admit that.

I told my agent I wanted to do some TV. She protested that it would tie me down. "That's the point," I told her. "Something has to."

Without Michael, I felt untethered. As if I had not only lost him but also myself. I still loved Michael but there was Hannah to think about now, not my brilliant career, not my broken heart. Numb, I went through with the divorce. Numb, I wanted to go back to work to stay numb.

My agent found me a job—a very good job—on a daytime soap. I went from being a sultry movie star to playing "Nurse Kelly"—a sultry soap star whose languid come-hither looks were outstripped only by her virtue. Nurse Kelly was the only regular on my show who never—*never*—got laid. Of course she didn't. She was suffering from unrequited love for Dr. McGowan. I could identify.

"Do you think you end up becoming your character?" a fanzine editor asked me three years into my run.

"Oh, no! I hope not!" I protested. Obviously, I had.

Who struck me Snow White? I wondered. There had to be one interesting man in Los Angeles. Everyone else managed to date— or commit serial matrimony. Instead, I managed to be a good mommy.

Patricia cleaned up, very publicly, begging everyone's forgiveness. Six months later, she published a mean-spirited book about what jerks all of us were.

"You should call her on it," my sister advised me. "Write your own book. Do something."

"I am doing something. I'm raising Hannah."

"You're a doormat!"

"I'm practicing non-resistance."

"Gandhi's dead," Linda told me. "And, in case your agent didn't tell you, Ben Kingsley got the role."

Hannah was eight the year my numbness finally melted. I cried deep, salty tears, nonstop, or so it seemed, for more than a year. They gave Nurse Kelly a death in her family to cover for me. Poor Nurse Kelly. She had a terrible time: tears and rage, rage and tears, tears and rage. I won an Emmy.

The day after the Emmy ceremonies, Linda told me she was going to get me a happy ending. All I had to do was get in the car and ride with her. She drove us to the Fairfax district, where a block was roped off for a street fair.

"What are we doing?" I protested.

"I want you to meet somebody."

Just what I needed. A fix-up with some carnie guy.

Linda dragged me to a booth where a little gray-haired lady sat next to a card table. She looked a lot like Mary Pickford or some other silent movie star, I couldn't remember just which.

"Sit down," Linda urged me. "She's incredible. I met her when her house got broken into."

I sat down. The little lady took my hand and cradled it between hers, which were incredibly soft and tiny.

"I see salty tears," she said. "Do you work in TV?"

"She's Nurse Kelly," Linda volunteered. "You've probably seen her."

"I'm sorry, sweetheart. I can't say that I have. I don't have a TV. I'm really a reader—but you're really a singer."

"What? I haven't sung in years. I never really sang. I mean, I did, but only because my husband needed me to."

"Well, now you need to. It'll do you a world of good."

With that, she turned to Linda. "So! You made detective!"

Linda made detective the next day. I decided it was her happy ending we had found there.

Hannah is a teenager now and she has reconciled with her father. In truth, she adores him. Who can blame her? He is Good Michael again. Hannah and Michael share holidays, summers, a love for movies and each other. Sometimes, coming home to me, she will tell me stories of the films she and her father screen together. I picture them happily cuddled up on the screening-room couch, munching away. Oh, yes. Hannah tells me they have a ritual of always making themselves fresh popcorn. She says her father is watching his weight these days and never touches salt.

I am not the first actress to parlay a career in acting into another in music. The year that Michael remarried—a young actress who looks remarkably like my former self—I began writing songs. No surprise that my songs, at first, were autobiographical. I was writing Michael out of my system:

> *Today I saw your picture.*
> *I found it in the papers.*
> *It was there for me—*
> *And a million other strangers.*

The album, which I called *Salty Tears*, won me Best New Female Vocalist and mildly astonished rave reviews. A little sheepishly, I find myself in possession of a double-barreled career. What's more, the singing award seemed to cheer up even Nurse Kelly. Oddly, when Nurse Kelly recovered from her grief, so did I.

It is no longer quite so painful for me that Hannah resembles her father more closely with every passing year. I can now talk to her about her father without having to force—or fight—my fondness. I tell her stories of "Good Michael," the man I will always love. But the song goes:

> *That was yesterday,*
> *And just like the papers,*
> *Some people throw it away.*

Acknowledgements

I want to thank my father, Jim Cameron, for driving me across Texas while I wrote these stories out longhand. I want to thank John Kane, my high school boyfriend and very first editor, for his topiary eye. I'd like to thank John Newland for laughing at my jokes and encouraging me to tell them. I'd like to thank Susan Schulman, my witty agent; Emma Lively-the name tells all; and most especially, Nina Wiener and Mari Florence for thinking this was a really great book.

About the Author

Julia Cameron has been an active artist for more than thirty years. She has extensive credits in film, television and theater. Her essays have been anthologized and she's a novelist and award-winning poet. Cameron has taught and refined the methods of her best-selling books on creativity, *The Artist's Way*, *The Vein of Gold* and *The Right to Write*, around the world for two decades. An award-winning journalist, she's written for such diverse publications as *The New York Times*, *The Washington Post*, *Rolling Stone*, and *Vogue*. For the past several years her focus has been on musicals, as both a writer and composer. Cameron lives in Taos, New Mexico and Venice, California.

Other Really Great Books

Plots and Characters: A Screenwriter on Screenwriting
Millard Kaufman
ISBN 1-893329-03-8, $24.95

The Jook: A Crime Novel
Gary Phillips
ISBN 1-893329-04-6, $12.95

*Hungry? A Guide to LA's Greatest Diners, Dives, Cafeterias,
and Coffee Shops!*
ISBN 1-893329-06-2, $12.95

*Thirsty? A Guide to LA's Greatest Coffeehouses, Juice Bars,
and Cocktail Bars!*
ISBN 1-893329-07-0, $12.95

Neutra Houses
with photographs by Julius Shulman, edited by Molly Siple
ISBN 1-893329-05-4, $35.00

Really Great Books
P.O. Box 861302
Los Angeles, CA 90086
USA

www.ReallyGreatBooks.com